"I don't think my brother would mind if you were planning on kissing me good-night—"

Rick whispered, his mouth almost on hers.

Cynthia was shocked. "I wasn't—"

"After all, we are practically family...."

"No."

"No?"

"No! I mean, yes, we are practically family, but no, I...I...don't...want...you...to...kiss me." She closed her eyes against the pull of Rick's glittering eyes and tried to will him into releasing her. Which was hard, as she wanted nothing of the kind.

However, what *he* wanted was something different altogether. Clearly, he wanted to punish her for committing what he perceived to be a crime against his family. He wanted to prove with a kiss that she really wasn't after his brother, but after his brother's money. What better way to demonstrate what he believed to be so obvious?

No. She could not let him kiss her. No matter how much she wanted him to.

Dear Reader,

Now that the holidays are over, I'll bet you need some serious R and R, and what better way to escape the everyday and recharge your spirit than with Silhouette Romance? We'll take you on the rewarding, romantic journey from courtship to commitment!

This month you're in for some very special surprises! First, beloved Carolyn Zane returns with *The Cinderella Inheritance* (#1636), a tender, rollicking, triumphant rags-to-riches love story. Then Karen Rose Smith brings you the next installment in the amazing SOULMATES series. In *With One Touch* (#1638), Brooke Pennington can magically heal animals, but only Dr. Nate Stanton has the power to cure her own aching heart.

If the greatest lesson in life is love, then you won't want to miss these two Romance novels. In Susan Meier's *Baby on Board* (#1639), the first in her DAYCARE DADS miniseries, Caro Evans is hired to teach dark, guarded Max Riley how to care for his infant daughter—and how to love again. And in *The Prince's Tutor* (#1640) by Nicole Burnham, Amanda Hutton is used to instructing royal *children* about palace protocol, but not a full-grown playboy prince with other lessons in mind....

Appearances can be deceiving, especially in Cathie Linz's *Sleeping Beauty & the Marine* (#1637), about journalist Cassandra Jones who loses the glasses and colors her hair to find out if gentlemen prefer blondes, and hopes a certain marine captain doesn't! Then former bad-boy Matt Webster nearly goes bananas when he agrees to be the pretend fiancé of one irresistible virgin, in Shirley Jump's *The Virgin's Proposal* (#1641).

Next month, look for popular Romance author Carla Cassidy's 50th book, part of a duo called THE PREGNANCY TEST, about two women with two very different test results!

Happy reading!

Mary-Theresa Hussey

Mary-Theresa Hussey
Senior Editor

Please address questions and book requests to:
Silhouette Reader Service
U.S.: 3010 Walden Ave., P.O. Box 1325, Buffalo, NY 14269
Canadian: P.O. Box 609, Fort Erie, Ont. L2A 5X3

Carolyn Zane

THE CINDERELLA INHERITANCE

SILHOUETTE *Romance*®

Published by Silhouette Books

America's Publisher of Contemporary Romance

For Sandy Steffen, author.
I'm quite certain we were separated at birth, as the coincidences in our
lives are simply too bizarre: the midlife braces, the Bettys, our darling
MJ, strange symptoms, life, death, writing, great kids, hunky
hubbies…and even though she inherited the inability to gain weight
during pregnancy, I still love her.

And for my precious readers:
The Lord bless thee and keep thee.

SILHOUETTE BOOKS

ISBN 0-373-19636-9

THE CINDERELLA INHERITANCE

Copyright © 2003 by Carolyn Suzanne Pizzuti

This edition published by arrangement with Harlequin Books S.A.

® and TM are trademarks of Harlequin Books S.A., used under license.
Trademarks indicated with ® are registered in the United States Patent
and Trademark Office, the Canadian Trade Marks Office and in other
countries.

Visit Silhouette at www.eHarlequin.com

Printed in U.S.A.

Books by Carolyn Zane

CAROLYN ZANE

lives with her husband, Matt, their preschool daughter, Madeline, and their latest addition, baby daughter Olivia, in the rolling countryside near Portland, Oregon's Willamette River. Like Chevy Chase's character in the movie *Funny Farm,* Carolyn finally decided to trade in a decade of city dwelling and producing local television commercials for the quaint country life of a novelist. And, even though they have bitten off decidedly more than they can chew in the remodeling of their hundred-plus-year-old farmhouse, life is somewhat saner for her than for poor Chevy. The neighbors are friendly, the mail carrier actually stops at the box and the dog, Bob Barker, sticks close to home.

Dear Reader,

As a child, I always wondered what happened during that nebulous period referred to as "ever after." "And they lived happily ever after" was simply not enough. What was the wedding like? Come on! Why didn't *we* ever get to go to the wedding? Snow White waves to us from the horse with her Prince Charming as they ride toward the castle…and then what? Beauty (from…*and the Beast*) dances around the ballroom with her guy, and we are given the rumblings of another "happily ever after"…but what does that *mean?* Cinderella rushes out of the church and waves to us…but I don't recall attending the wedding. How can we be sure any of them actually ever married?

And, if they didn't get married, what is Snow White up to these days? I'd imagine what with her skills at organization and managing numbers of men, she's now the CEO of a major corporation. And Beauty? With her love of books, an author no doubt. Probably writing romances for Silhouette Romance. Probably married to some guy named Matt (not that he's a beast, mind you, unless he's watching a game—and then stand back). Probably has a couple of kids, couple of dogs, piles of laundry and dishes, cars that break down, bills to pay… You know, your typical "ever after."

And Cinderella? Well, now. If you want to know the *real* story behind *her* wedding, just keep turning the pages.

Best always,

Carolyn Zane

www.carolynzane.com

Chapter One

From behind an arrangement of white lilies, Cynthia Noble watched her fiancé, Graham Wingate, dart a covert glance around the room before he sidled up to the legal assistant and began to flirt. The blond bombshell with large bedroom eyes and come-hither smile emitted an animal magnetism that was hard to ignore.

The young legal assistant was rather attractive, as well.

Cynthia sighed.

And this randy behavior at his grandfather's funeral wake, no less. Would Graham ever grow up? She dropped her face into her hands and gave her temples a vicious rub. Doubtful, knowing him. His flirtatious antics were part of his charm and one of the many reasons she'd been attracted to Graham in the first place. He was charismatic, smart, hardworking, gorgeous, funny and fun loving.

Everything but faithful.

And that was becoming a bit of a problem.

With aching feet Cynthia moved to the front doors of the Seattle Heights Wingate Manor and continued going through the motions of thanking and bidding farewell to those who'd gathered there to honor Graham's grandfather, Alfred Wingate, millionaire, philanthropist and all-around prince of a guy. Graham's mother, Katherine, something of an easily bruised Southern peach, lay wilted upon an old-fashioned fainting couch in the parlor, just off the grand foyer, too overcome by her father-in-law's recent passing to perform her hostess duties.

So, as Cynthia still considered herself to be in Alfred's employ as his personal assistant until the end of this day, it was up to her to be strong.

She held out her hand to old Mrs. Meier, heir to the Meier peppermint fortune. Or the "mint-mint" as her social circle liked to joke. "I'm so very glad you could make it today, Mrs. M."

"Wouldn't have missed it for the world." Gnarled fingers fumbled with the brooch at her throat. "Alfred Wingate cut quite the dashing figure of a man when he was young. He used to come calling, back before he met Jayne."

"His wife was Elaine," Cynthia gently corrected.

"Ehh?"

"Elaine. Again, it was lovely to see you."

"Thank you, darlin', but my name is Martha."

Cynthia stretched a patient smile over her teeth as she held the door for Mrs. Meier and her chauffeur. A blustery wind blew in off the shores of Lake Washington, whipping their skirts and hair and sending leaves scudding down the lane. In the distance the Seattle skyline stood in stark contrast against the blackening sky. A Pacific storm was brewing and Cynthia was glad that the staff had banked the fires.

As she bid farewell to the rest of the elite circle of Wingate cronies, she decided that the home fires might not have needed stoking after all. For in her peripheral vision she could see things heating up between Graham and his new "friend." Hand against the wall, he had his quarry cornered, his pearly whites flashing as his low laughter rumbled forth. Her shoulders thrown back, the legal assistant arched against him, all lazy eyes and pouty lips and bulging body parts.

Exhaustion had Cynthia's normally square shoulders flagging a bit.

Thank heavens this was nearly over.

All of it.

For the past month Cynthia had been through the wringer, trying to hold everything together for Alfred's sake. But soon, within the next few hours, in fact, she would be on her own again. Just her against the world.

The thought both excited and frightened her. Cynthia hated being alone. But even more, she hated duplicity. And her engagement to Graham was becoming a sham that simply could not go on. She'd tell him before the day ended. Later they could figure out a way to break the news to his parents. Then they could get on with the business of their separate lives.

She sighed as another peek in his direction told her that Graham would have much less trouble getting back into the swing than she would.

No matter.

She'd find ways to stay busy. She had school. And her new part-time job. And...her dog. Pulling her lower lip between her teeth, she bit down and fought off the eternal longing that plagued her, for someone to call her own. A love such as it was rumored her mother and father had shared when they were alive.

At last the remaining guests departed with hugs and pats and murmurs of sympathy that left Cynthia teary and emotional. For in losing Alfred, she had lost not just her employer, but her mentor. Her family.

When the door was shut for the final time, a member of the legal team held up a crystal wine goblet and gave it several taps with a silver knife for the benefit of those who remained by invitation only.

"Ladies and gentlemen, the time has come for us to commence the reading of the will. Will those of you who were asked to stay please join us in the library?"

As the attorney and his staff prepared for the reading, many of Alfred's shirttail relatives and fair-weather friends roamed about the luxurious baronial library, peering at photos and priceless mementos and waxing poetic about the old man. All were hoping to be remembered in the will.

"Alfred was such a wonderful man."

"A philanthropist."

"A patron of the arts."

"An encourager."

"Generous."

"Loving."

"A veritable saint."

A frown furrowed Cynthia's brow. Where were all these people when the loving, generous, veritable saint was sick and dying this past year? With the lone exception of herself and Graham's parents, he'd been all but forgotten up here on the hill in this cavernous mansion, visited only when business and social protocol demanded.

She swallowed against the lump in her throat as she moved through the rows of folding chairs set up in the library and found a seat in the back. Graham, red faced and smelling faintly of perfume, joined her and took her hand. As she returned his light squeeze, she suddenly understood that the thing she enjoyed most about her relationship with Graham was his family.

First and foremost, of course, his grandfather Alfred.

Also firmly entrenched in her affections were Graham's

slightly offbeat parents, the befuddled Harrison and the fragile Katherine.

Head bowed, Cynthia battled back the tears and could scarcely bear to think about how much she'd miss them all. All, that is, with the lone exception of Graham's older brother, Rick. She had yet to meet this ill-mannered globe-trotter, but if the lack of respect he'd shown Alfred by ignoring his death and subsequent funeral were any indication, she'd pass.

Rick Wingate set his duffel bag on the black-and-white-checkered marble floor in the entrance of his grandfather's house and shut the door behind him. Outside, the wind howled something fierce and he thanked his lucky stars that he'd made it home before they'd closed the airport. Inside, the foyer was strangely devoid of humanity. Hushed. Even the servants were missing, although the lights blazed and the air was cozy and smelled of fresh coffee.

He dragged his hands through his longish hair. A glance in the huge gilt mirror near the entry had him wishing he'd taken the time to get a haircut. As usual, Murphy's Law had absconded with his well-laid plans. Silently he cursed the storm that had delayed his connection. Because of it, he'd missed his grandfather's funeral and the wake that followed. He'd wanted to be here to honor the man who'd had such a profound impact on his life—more than just about anything. With a heavy sigh he stuffed his shirttails inside his jeans and did his best to make himself present-able.

From the library, he could hear voices and deduced that he was arriving just as the reading of the will was beginning. Quietly he let himself in through the door. A balding lawyer type was standing before Alfred's remarkable hand-carved desk, clutching a ream of papers and exuding sympathy.

"—want to thank you all for being here today. I know that this is a difficult time for you...."

As unobtrusively as possible, Rick moved to a secluded spot behind a giant potted palm by the door and watched the crowd nod and dab at their eyes. He swallowed a snort of disgust. With the exception of his mother and father, most of these bottom feeders were here for the money and likely hadn't seen Alfred in years. He scratched the stubble at his jaw. Not that he could talk. Last time he'd seen Alfred was Christmas, two years ago. But at least *he* wasn't here to turn an infernal buck.

"—his generosity. And so it is with great sorrow that we divide his many personal effects and assets...."

Rick's gaze strayed to his mother as she lay slumped against his father's sloping shoulders. Her nose was shiny red and her pallor paler than usual. Spotting him, his mother lifted a wilted hand, and he smiled and nodded and indicated that he'd visit with them after this was over. Though they were dotty and eccentric, Rick knew that his parents would miss the crotchety old man. Their grief was genuine.

Unlike the pseudosomber expression his brother wore. Graham was self-absorption personified and was no doubt mentally calculating the quarterly earnings on his projected inheritance.

"—and so I'll begin with the various stock holdings." The lawyer adjusted the reading glasses perched at the tip of his bulbous nose. "To my son, Harrison, I, Alfred Wingate, being of sound mind, do hereby bequeath five hundred thousand shares of Systems Points West—"

Tuning out, Rick let his gaze travel to the softly sobbing beauty who clutched his brother's hand. Graham's intended. He bit his lip to forestall the sneer that threatened.

This was the first time, other than the pictures his mother had sent, that he'd laid eyes on her.

"—two hundred and fifty thousand shares to be divided by my nephews, Roger, Theodore and Bradley—"

Like all of Graham's previous fiancées, she was a looker. Far more attractive in person than in the snapshots he'd seen. From where he stood, he could see that she wore her light brown hair upswept and tidy, unlike the usual blond messes that attracted Graham. About her slender throat she wore an old-fashioned cameo choker and her clothing was somber and tasteful.

Rick frowned. Odd.

As his gaze swept over her shapely legs and hips and on up to her face, he figured she must have felt his scrutiny, because she turned to glance in his direction. Dropping back behind the palm's lacy foliage, he was struck by the eerie almost white-blue color of her eyes. They were incredible. Otherworldly. Riveting. They were without a doubt the largest, lightest—almost transparent—eyes he'd ever seen. She was memorable, all right.

How this one had managed to hang in with his brother's womanizing ways for an entire year was anyone's guess. Must need the money. Otherwise she'd have been out of here long ago.

Just like all the rest.

"—my darling daughter-in-law, Katherine, whom I adore, I leave all holdings in my transatlantic—"

Rick tugged at a palm frond to get a better look at Cynthia's elegant profile. He watched her blow her nose and scrub at her cheeks with a monogrammed scrap of lace. Strange, he mused. This time, his brother's fiancée held an air of class about her. A regal bearing that spoke of breeding and pedigree. *Dignified,* was the word that came to mind. Unusual characteristics for an unscrupulous gold digger, but then it took all kinds to make a world, he decided with derision.

"—to be split equally between my grandsons, Richard and Graham Wingate."

Absently Rick tuned back in and wondered what it was that he'd just inherited, but he didn't really care. He'd always taken care of himself. Prided himself on being the independent one in the family. The one who knew there was more to life than croissants for breakfast and a ten-o'clock tee time.

"—which concludes the division of liquid assets. Okay. So. Now I'll move on to the physical property." The lawyer shuffled through his papers, cleared his throat, adjusted his glasses and gazed dramatically at the audience before he began to read.

"To my future granddaughter-in-law, Cynthia Noble," he boomed, "I leave Wingate Manor—"

After a collective gasp of shock, silence reigned.

"And its acreage, staff, furniture and complete contents, including the paintings, sculptures, cars, outbuildings, flora, fauna, et cetera, along with a considerable trust account to be used in its care, maintenance, staff salaries and other miscellany." The lawyer pulled off his specs and gnawed on the stem in a worried fashion, seeming to know this wouldn't sit well.

His upper lip curling, Rick settled back against the wall to watch it all head for the fan.

Narrowed eyes grew accusatory as people twisted in their seats to stare at Cynthia, who was honking into her handkerchief, oblivious to what had just transpired. The air grew thick and murmurings swelled.

"Why," one hawk-nosed second cousin muttered, "she's not even related."

"Yet," another beady-eyed great-uncle-in-law groused.

"Just who is she, anyway? Certainly her family is no-body special, or we'd have heard of her."

"Well," a maiden aunt said, sniffing, "one need only look at her to know why Alfred left her the house."

Rick frowned as the rumblings took a decided turn for the nasty.

"Alfred was such a dodo."

"Delusional."

"Mean-spirited."

"Drunk."

"Obviously besotted by a young girl."

Rick turned his attention back to Cynthia. Head back, scrunched eyes leaking, she hiccuped noisily, seemingly clueless of the animosity directed at her. She was quite a little actress.

Graham nudged her, his grin broad as the Cheshire cat on holiday. Her head lolled, watery eyes to his, and blinked quizzically.

"What?" she mouthed.

"You just inherited the house."

"The house? What house?"

"This house."

"What?" Cynthia's jaw hung open.

Katherine fumbled with the lid on a bottle of nerve pills. Her voice was breathy as she said, "Surely there must be some mistake."

"Dad couldn't have been serious," a perplexed Harrison put forth, his eyes round with wonder beneath his bottle-bottom lenses.

Together Graham's parents turned around in their seats and graced Cynthia with feeble smiles.

"No offense, darlin'," Katherine whispered on a sigh, "but we are shocked and disappointed to say the least. All my married life I'd counted on one day moving up here to the manor on the hill. And now…" She slumped back against Harrison's bony rib cage and her eyes fluttered shut.

"I—I—I don't know what to say," Cynthia murmured, blanching white as the lilies that filled the room.

"Try thank you." Rick stepped away from the door, his voice dripping with sarcasm. "You're rich."

Cynthia turned her dazed expression to him and for a microsecond he thought he saw a flash of hurt beneath those pale blue eyes. Nah. All part of the act. Like Graham, she was probably calculating her profits.

"Certainly this cannot hold up in a court of law," came Harrison's genteel protestation. "After all—" again he twisted to peer at Cynthia, causing Katherine to droop even farther into his lap "—we can't be certain that your relationship with Graham will last." He was flushed and perspiring, his lopsided grin weak. "In that unfortunate event, the house might not stay in the family. Not that we don't think of you as family already, dear one. But you can surely understand our reservations."

Cynthia turned her dull gaze on Harrison and nodded.

The attorney struggled to loosen the silk knot at his throat. "Actually, Harrison, Alfred was quite—" he groped for the words that would politely express Alfred's penchant for swearing a blue streak "—er, *adamant* about having Cynthia inherit the Wingate mansion, rather than members of his immediate family. He had his reasons and wanted us all to respect them. In fact—" He fumbled through his papers. "Uh…you should all know that the will goes on to stipulate that if she chooses not to accept this gift, that the house and its entire contents must be given to the nonprofit charity of her choice."

"Wha…?" Katherine and Harrison stared agog, babbling. "Bu… Tha… *Wha?*"

The lawyer held up his copy of the will. "Sorry about that. And Cynthia, even if you wanted to give the house back to the family—'' the family turned hopeful eyes upon her ''—the will is airtight. I know. I wrote it.''

Rick watched as Cynthia—elbows to knees—leaned forward and dropped her head into her hands. Gripped in the throes of some indefinable emotion, she pitched about, shoulders bobbing.

He gave his head a rueful shake. Great show.

No doubt she was laughing all the way to the bank.

''Excuse me.'' Cynthia bared her teeth in a pseudosmile at the voluptuous legal assistant and wedged her way between the girl and Graham. ''I won't keep him, I promise.''

Truer words were never spoken.

With grim determination Cynthia grabbed Graham's hand and tugged him from the ensuing post-will-reading fray to a quiet spot in the foyer, just outside the library doors.

''We need to talk.''

''I'll say.'' Graham grinned and pulled her close. ''Congrats on getting us the house, babe. Way to go.''

''Way to go?'' Cynthia stared at him. ''*Way to go?* Just what, exactly, are you trying to say?'' Is *that* why he thought she spent so much time in his grandfather's company? To *get* them the house?

A puzzled frown joined his brows. ''Uh—''

''Is that lipstick on your jaw?''

First his neck grew blotchy red, then his cheeks. ''Oh, uh—''

''Ohhh, *Grahammmm.*'' Cynthia exhaled his name on a long, slow groan. ''Never mind. Listen.'' She held her breath and counted to ten before she spoke. ''I think the time has come for us to end this charade of an engagement.''

''What? But I—''

"Don't act so surprised. You've been catting around for months now."

"Are you talking about her?" He flicked a thumb over his shoulder at the legal assistant, then rolled his eyes and blew a little raspberry between his grinning lips. "Ah, c'mon, I was just clowning around."

"Yes, I know," she hissed. "And for Alfred's sake I've put up with it because, for some reason, knowing that I was going to be part of his family made him happy. But we have to accept the fact that Alfred is gone now and so are any chances that we'll ever marry."

"Oh, and so now that he's dead, you're going to just take your money and run, is that it?" A faintly unpleasant curl changed the tenor of Graham's mouth. The electronic strains of "We're in the Money" chimed from his breast pocket. Graham's voice grew mellifluous as he retrieved his phone. "Graham Wingate here."

Cynthia would not be dissuaded by his endless business dealings and tugged at his sleeve. "That's not fair. I had no idea what was in that will."

Her heated whisper had Graham covering the mouthpiece with his palm.

"Yeah, right. Listen, can we talk about this later?"

"We can talk about this *now,* buster!" Cynthia grabbed his hand and pulled his phone to her mouth. "Mr. Wingate will have to call you back. Goodbye." She jabbed at the off button, concluding the phone call.

Graham leveled a look at her that she'd never seen before. A look that no doubt drove terror into the hearts of those he ran over in his daily business dealings. "Cynthia, this is no time to make such a monumental decision. Besides, this house is as much mine as it is yours."

"Only if we marry. And Graham, I don't see that happening without benefit of a shotgun."

"Cynthia, this selfish streak is definitely unflattering."

Again the phone played its tune and Graham was instantly charming. "Graham Wingate here. Can you hold one moment? Thank you." To Cynthia he snapped, "You know, of course, that this will kill my parents. They love you."

Ah. *They* loved her. No word about *his* feelings. Cynthia's molars ground together. Typical.

Together they glanced into the library. From where they stood, she and Graham could both see his parents chatting with the lawyer. They were clutching each other and swaying in a nonexistent breeze, still shell-shocked at the outcome of the reading.

"They…will come to understand." She pinched her lower lip, knowing that even as she spoke, telling them the truth about their canceled engagement would be like telling Mr. Rogers that she didn't want to be his neighbor. "Eventually."

"No, they won't. This estate is the Wingate signature property. It's been in the family for nearly a century. And now you're just going to steal away with our history?"

Jaw jutting, she stared at his skeptical expression in outrage. She'd actually been planning to *marry* this brute?

To the phone he said, "Sorry about the interruption. Please continue." Frowning, Graham glanced at his watch. "Tonight? Of course. Sure. Boston…let's see…" He pulled his PalmPilot out of his pocket and quickly scanned his calendar. "Okay…yes. What time is the flight?"

"You're not going to fly off on one of your endless business trips until we iron this out!" she shrieked, and— feeling the hairs on the back of her neck begin to tingle— turned to see the man Katherine had introduced earlier as Graham's older brother, Rick, staring curiously at them from across the library.

He was the smart aleck who'd taunted her about being rich.

She shot him a ferocious smile that warned him to mind

his own damn business and was irked by the insolence in his answering grin. How had the mild, unassuming Harrison and Katherine given birth to two such arrogant sons? And, where she'd instantly taken a shine to Graham when they'd met, it was hate at first sight for this reproving, holier-than-thou Rick character.

She could tell by his self-satisfied smirk that he was judging her without benefit of a trial. In her, he no doubt saw a moneygrubbing harridan, harping on his brother, even as she made off with the family fortune.

As he crossed his beefy, tattooed arms over his disgustingly muscular chest and cocked a narrow hip against a credenza, she had to wonder if he was adopted, for he certainly didn't bear any resemblance to the rest of the Wingate gene pool. She glanced at Graham, who was tall and slender and fair and rather pretty for a man. The two brothers were like night and day. Where one was smooth and urbane, the other was primitive and obviously lacking the Wingate social graces.

And the bony crones who wobbled around the library and made up the rest of the family tree? They all looked as if a wafting feather would topple them like a set of rotted dominoes.

Her eyes refocused on Rick. Yes. Had to have been switched at birth. This guy was rough around the edges. Dark. Swarthy. Sort of menacing. He gave her the creeps.

Spinning on the heels of her pumps, she turned her back on him and growled at Graham, who was, unbelievably, still in the middle of closing yet another international real estate deal.

"Graham!"

Hand over the phone's mouthpiece, he barked, "Cynthia, let it alone. You're not feeling yourself. Under the circumstances, I forbid you to tell my mother that you are calling off our engagement right now. With her fragile psyche, she's been through enough shock this last week to set her back in therapy for at least two years. As it is, she is on every kind of nerve pill ever invented. And—'' he glowered at her ''—hearing that I'm ending yet another engagement would send her over the edge for sure. I'm not kidding when I say this would kill her.''

Cynthia shot a wary glance at Katherine, whom she adored. It was true. The woman was delicacy incarnate, preferring to view the world through her rose-colored glasses, as the reality of life often proved too much to bear. Unfortunately, Graham was right. This would kill her.

''Fine. We can inform them of our breakup later. As soon as you get back from your business trip. How long are you going to be gone?''

Graham consulted the party on the other end of the line. After bidding them goodbye, he said, ''Two weeks to put the paperwork together in the States, and a week in Europe, so a few weeks at the most.''

''*A few weeks!*'' Chin to shoulder, she caught Rick watching them and knew that he found their conversation both fascinating and amusing. She snapped her head around and lowered her voice. She could feel the veins fairly bulging in her neck. ''You can't be gone for nearly a month!''

''Cynthia.'' He tilted his head and bestowed a condescending smile on her. ''You have been under an incredible amount of pressure lately. A month apart may do us some good. I promise you, after you've had some time to grieve and adjust, things will seem a lot better and then you and I can sort everything out and get back to where we were.''

''No, Graham. It is you who need to adjust. We are *not* going to marry. Never. Do you understand? Our engagement is off.''

Graham's head dipped, and for a moment Cynthia was

tempted to feel sorry for him. Telling his parents that he'd failed at yet another romance was going to be hard on his extraordinarily large ego.

He rallied. "We'll just see."

"Yes. We'll just see."

"Fine."

"Fine."

"Fine."

"Fine."

"And the thing of it is—" Cynthia poured a glass of milk for herself and one for Rosy Cheeks, then ripped open a box of cookies "—I don't even *want* the stupid house."

She pitched a cookie onto the kitchen floor and stared vacantly as her bulldog chased it across the linoleum with her protruding lower teeth. Like a deranged hockey player, the dog grunted and slid, scrambling after her edible puck.

Though she was exhausted, Cynthia hadn't been able to sleep that night. So instead of lying in bed—continuously replaying the bizarre reading of the will over in her mind— she'd decided to tackle some unfinished craft projects.

Her cramped studio apartment didn't afford much room for a work area, but Cynthia didn't mind. Stacks of unfinished Creative Memory pages featuring Rosy Cheeks and her on vacation littered one cardboard table. Another was cluttered with glitter and beads and painting projects and glue guns galore and the scraps she'd been meaning to quilt for less fortunate families. Another corner was strewn with a half-painted chest of drawers, some pillows in the process of being cross-stitched, a pile of bargain fabric ready to be turned into curtains and everything she needed to solder a stained-glass lampshade into a Tiffany knockoff.

Cynthia figured that although she might not have a family, at least her abode should be homey. Tightly budgeted, she prided herself on being able to turn flea-market finds into treasures with a fresh coat of paint and a little creativity. And her place reflected her abilities to turn a dump—with a few flower arrangements and pillows and candles—into a magazine spread.

After a bit of rummaging, she picked up her knitting to begin work on the tiny yellow sweater she was making for a co-worker's baby, and took a seat at her overflowing kitchen table.

"And, Rosy-girl, here's the catch-22. The family would have a cow if I gave Alfred's house to a nonprofit organization. But after I break up with Graham, they'll have a cow if I keep it."

Pushing aside a stack of college texts, unopened mail and a packet of paperwork that Alfred's lawyer had tucked into her hands, Cynthia propped her knitting bag on the tiny tabletop. Needles clicking, she watched Rosy Cheeks finally corner her cookie. Like a canine food processor, she chopped it to bits, flinging crumbs under the table and snorting in a way that made Cynthia imagine the dog was laughing.

"Yeah, right. To you it's funny. To me…it's a nightmare. It was very sweet of Alfred to hold me in such high regard, but honestly! I don't think he thought this thing all the way through. However, I think I have a way to solve this whole mess," she mused.

An attentive Rosy Cheeks licked her chops, swabbed her nostrils and gave her tail a few "feed-me" thumps.

"Yep, it's the only way, really." She tossed Rosy Cheeks a dog biscuit and the dog sniffed it, batted it away and then sat wriggling, thinking Cynthia had made a mistake. "That's it. I'll simply join the witness protection program. Change my name. My address. My appearance…"

Dragging a hand over her face, she emitted some strangled laughter.

"No? Okay. I'll just call Katherine now, and let her know that I'm turning the mansion into a halfway house." She picked up her phone and waved it around. "I'll beg her forgiveness, and then next month I'll rip her heart out with the news that I'm not marrying her son." She groaned long and loud. "Ohhhhh, Ieee *hate* this! Rosy, what on earth could Alfred have been thinking, leaving me all this…this…*stuff*?"

Cynthia flopped dramatically forward and, in the process, knocked her knitting and paperwork on the floor and sent Rosy Cheeks scuttling. "Sorry, girl." Hanging over the edge of her chair, she snagged the scattered stack and thunked it back atop the table.

"What's this?" she murmured, picking up an envelope that had her name scrawled in Alfred's spidery handwriting. Must have fallen out of the lawyer's envelope. Immediately her eyes welled with tears. She stood and moved to the living-room area and the futon that served as her couch as well as her bed. A golden glow filled the small room as she snapped on the light and settled back against a stack of pleasantly color-coordinated pillows. Rosy Cheeks jumped up beside her and settled her jowls over Cynthia's thigh.

"Alfred," Cynthia murmured, and swiped at the tears with her knuckles, "y'old goat. What now?"

Sliding a nail under the flap, she broke the seal, withdrew a letter and began to read.

My darling girl,
Since you are reading this missive, it's safe to assume that I'm gone and the vultures have flown in, picked up their spoils and headed out. I imagine you are feeling a bit dazed by your windfall, but I have my reasons, so hear me out before you pick up the phone to

call Katherine and Harrison and tell them you're turning the place into a home for vagrants.

Cynthia hiccuped and laughed and wiped her eyes on her sleeve. Even now he understood her thoughts.

I have three very important reasons that I'm leaving the house to you.

Number one reason: I was the one that talked you into going back to college. Since you wouldn't let me help you finance your tuition—and I respect you for that—I must insist upon helping you with room and board. I acknowledge that Wingate Manor is a bit much for a college student, but imagine the parties! Rent out rooms to other students. Scandalize this stuffy neighborhood.

Number two reason: I built this place for my first love and our family and, when we did not marry because of circumstances beyond our control, I was devastated. You remind me of her, my dear. More than you'll ever know. There is nothing that would make me happier than to know that you are here, caring for and enjoying my special home.

Number three reason: I know that you are planning to marry my grandson. It is my hope that this house will be the dowry that your family was unable to provide and doubly knot you to the Wingate clan. Cynthia dear, everyone needs a family, and you've gone far too long without. I loved you like a granddaughter, and am certain that if my true love and I had married, our granddaughter would have looked just like you. Cynthia, my child, I love you as if you were my own. You made these last months of my life the happiest since I was your own age. Please keep my gift. I

promise it will bring you happiness equal to that
which you have brought to me.

For always,
Your loving grandfather-in-law,
Alfred Wingate

Tears streamed down Cynthia's face as her eyes roved
over the shaky penmanship. She'd never known her own
grandparents. In fact, after the age of three she'd never
even known her own parents. Alfred knew how losing her
own family at such an early age had haunted her. He'd
mentioned more than once that in losing his precious first
love to an arranged marriage, he'd lost a family, too.

"Oh, Alfred."

Bowed forelegs wobbling, Rosy Cheeks stood up on
Cynthia's thigh and licked her face. Then, snuffling in her
ear, she made little grunts of sympathy. Cynthia pulled the
full-bellied dog into her lap and squeezed. "You are the
sister I never had," she murmured, and received a noseful
of slobber for her sentiment.

She stared at the pages she held in her free hand, more
confused now than ever before. Should she keep the
house? Should she give it away? The doorbell's sudden
blast startled her and set Rosy Cheeks to barking.

Cynthia hesitated. Who would be calling on her at this
hour? Graham was out of town and any other people she
considered close friends were still in Duluth, Minnesota,
where she'd lived before coming to work for Alfred.

"Who is it?" Caution in her step, she approached the
door and squinted through the peephole. It was too dark
in the hall to make out more than a burly shadow.

"It's me, Rick Wingate. Graham's brother. May I come
in for a moment to speak with you?"

Chapter Two

A lone lightbulb lit the dank and dingy hallway of the Elliott Bay Apartment complex, barely illuminating Cynthia's name as it was scrawled on the mail slot in her door. He'd searched for her unit in several buildings before finding her here. The laugh track of a TV sitcom ebbed and flowed from an apartment down the hall, and from above, a colicky baby shrieked, making it hard for Rick to be sure that she'd heard him the first time.

"Rick Wingate, your soon-to-be brother-in-law," he explained for good measure, and then peered through the peephole trying to decide if he had the right place after all.

Over all of this, a mother bickered with her teenaged son, and a door slammed so hard the windows rattled. The smells of fried fish, musty carpet and wet animal lay heavily upon the air. As he stood outside Cynthia's apartment, listening to her dog sounding a ferocious battle cry, he had to wonder if coming over here had been such a brilliant idea after all.

But curiosity had gotten the better of him after that scene between his brother and her, back at the Wingate Manor. He'd witnessed his brother's advances toward the buxom legal assistant when Graham thought Cynthia wasn't looking. And the times she'd noticed his shenanigans, she didn't really seem to care.

What was up with that?

He guessed inheriting millions in property and assets made up for Graham's crass indiscretions. And now Graham was flying off on business for an entire month, just hours after they'd cleaned up at the reading of the will. Interesting. Didn't necessarily mean anything. Then again... he smelled a rat.

Every time he'd approached his sister-in-law-to-be after the reading and tried to strike up a conversation, she'd been evasive. Hiding something. Her too-bright smile and guilty demeanor had irritated him as she'd backed away. Deceit did not sit well with Rick. He'd never liked it in Graham, and he liked it even less in this Cynthia woman.

When he'd gone back to his parents' spacious home in an upscale Seattle suburb he'd tried to worm some information out of his mother, although, as usual, she was too fatigued to be much help. He'd followed Katherine to her room and perched on the edge of her bed as she'd lain there with a cold cloth on her head. Glancing about the opulent room, he'd thought about the squalor within which he'd lived for the past two years and gave his head a single shake. People here had no idea how spoiled they were.

"It's so good to have you home." Katherine's voice was feeble as she flopped a hand upon his knee. "You're looking robust. Somewhat shaggy and unkempt perhaps, but healthy nevertheless."

"I wish I could say the same for you." Rick lifted her wrist and took her pulse. A little thready. Leaning forward, he touched her forehead. Cool. "How have you been feeling?"

"Tired. As usual."

"What meds does your doctor have you on?"

"Just some tranquilizers and antidepressants. And a few sleep aids. A little blood-pressure thing and some heart pills. Nothing serious."

Katherine could see the cogs turning in his mind. "Darling, could you stop being a doctor for a minute and simply chat with me?"

Reining in his instincts to lecture, he gave her hand an affectionate pat. "Sure. What's new with you?"

"Nothing. Tell me about yourself." She dragged the damp cloth off her face and looked at him with a spark of interest. "Met any nice girls over there in...what is the name of that place you've been living again? I can never remember."

"Punjipur. It's a small village in northwestern India. They suffered a massive earthquake last Christmas. I've been helping out there for nearly a year now. Before that, several other small villages you've never heard of in northeastern Africa. Treating malnutrition."

Katherine did her best to swallow her dismay. "Oh. That's...good."

"Mmm-hmm. It really is. Recently I've been part of a newly formed traveling medical effort called the West Coast Emergency Medical Teams. We're sponsored by several philanthropic organizations around the world. And, no. I haven't had time to date. Even if I did, all the girls I meet are either sick, pregnant or injured and don't speak a whole lot of English. It makes for a rather stilted conversation." He grinned and rubbed her hand.

"I suppose it would," she agreed in a despondent tone, and then forced a bright smile. "Never mind. Your brother has taken the heat off you for a while, by becoming engaged to a wonderful girl. They have yet to set a wedding date, but I don't really see any reason for them to wait now that Cynthia has—'' a forlorn expression glanced across her face ''—inherited Alfred's mansion.''

The muscles that ran from Rick's neck up and through his jaw flexed. ''So I hear.''

''We always knew that Alfred was taken with her. We just didn't know how much.''

Oh, Alfred had been taken, all right. ''She was his assistant?''

''For this last year, yes. In fact, it was Alfred who suggested Graham ask Cynthia out for a date. It was love at first sight for them both.''

Rick forced his lips up at the corners and swallowed a groan. Sure. Love at first sight. Graham loved her leggy figure, and she loved his bankbook figures.

''Your father and I were delighted, considering Graham's rather sketchy engagement record. We were beginning to wonder if he was ever going to find a nice girl and settle down.'' She rotated her head and cocked a speculative brow at Rick.

He ignored the implied suggestion that they were also wondering about his marital status. ''So. Where did this Cynthia person come from?''

''Originally? Minnesota. She has no family, poor thing. Her parents died in a house fire when she was no more than a toddler. She was raised in foster care and state institutions until she graduated from high school.''

Rick gnawed the inside of his cheek. A likely story. Poor little orphan girl plays on an old man's heartstrings. Feigning horror, he squinted at his mother. ''You're allowing an uneducated—and even worse, an unpedigreed—girl to marry your son? Have you gone soft in your dotage?''

''After so many embarrassing breakups with the daughters of our good friends, I've become less...choosy. Besides, she's quite lovely."

All con artists were lovely until they ripped you off.

"And she's not uneducated. She's attending college."

"What is she studying?"

"Foreign languages. Wants to be an interpreter."

That would come in handy when setting up one's Swiss bank accounts. "How did she meet Grandpa?"

"I don't really know. I believe I once heard Alfred say that he was acquainted with her grandparents."

"Where does she live now?"

"Over by the university campus at the Elliott Bay Apartments."

That was weird. If he remembered correctly from his undergrad days, that complex was a veritable ghetto.

"Graham is dating a girl who lives at the Elliott Bay Apartments? Really?"

"Yes. She's very independent. Won't take a penny from anybody unless she's earned it. She's very proud. Alfred mentioned that she came from a fine family, but they're all gone now."

Katherine had rubbed her head and, sensing her fatigue after such an emotional day, Rick had bid her good-night and headed over to the Elliott Bay Apartments to find some answers for himself.

But now that he was here, looking at the graffiti that adorned the outside of her front door, he began to have a few qualms.

What was he going to say to her?

What did he want to know?

Just why the hell was he here?

Rick Wingate?

It took a moment for Cynthia to compute that Graham's odious brother was actually in her hallway. What on earth was *he* doing here?

She hesitated.

Then, deciding she couldn't hide forever, she pulled open her door. There he stood, wearing that same derisive smile he'd worn at the funeral. Her lips pruned at the sudden acid taste in her mouth.

"Hello." It was more of a curse than a greeting.

"Hi. I hope it isn't…too late?"

For what? She shrugged and made no move to invite him in.

"Are you going to invite me in?"

Was he kidding?

Slowly her eyes cruised over the shaggy brown hair, the small earring in his left ear, the dark stubble on his jaw, the leather jacket slung over his shoulder, the snug black T-shirt, the worn Levi's, the heavy work books, the motorcycle helmet that dangled from his free hand and the thorny tattoo that encircled his bulging biceps, and her first impulse was to slam the door in his face. He looked as if he'd just escaped from the county jail.

The only hint of civilization was his blindingly white, orthodontically correct smile. That and the fact that he smelled of some kind of manly deodorant.

But being that he was Alfred's grandson, she guessed she owed him the benefit of the doubt. Knotting the sash of her robe a bit more snugly over her ratty sweat suit, Cynthia stepped back and held the door open.

"I guess," she muttered.

"Gee. Thanks."

There was that sarcasm again.

She leaned against the door after she'd pushed it closed and watched him take in her tiny digs. His curious gaze traveled over the charming, tole-painted wooden cable spool she used as a coffee table to the Broadway play posters on the wall to the foofy futon with the piles of pillows, where Rosy Cheeks eyed him with suspicion.

"Nice place."

"Thanks."

"Live here long?"

"'Bout a year."

"Ah."

"Ah what? You seem surprised at something."

"I just thought my grandfather would have you living…I don't know…closer to him, I guess."

"I think I'm insulted on about a dozen different levels."

"Sorry." He didn't sound a bit sorry.

For a long moment they stood in silence until Cynthia could stand it no longer.

"So. Why are you here?"

"You're going to be my sister-in-law. I figured it was time we met."

"We met at the funeral."

"Yes, but we don't really know each other. You going to offer me something to drink?"

"No."

"That's okay. I brought refreshments." He nudged her out of the way, yanked open the door and, reaching into the hall, pulled a six-pack of beer from the floor just outside her apartment.

He slammed the door behind him with the heel of his boot. Taking two giant steps, he dropped the box of frosty bottles on her little spool table. "Beer?"

"No."

He ignored her and snagged one for each of them. Twisting off the tops, he held out a bottle. She watched him take a sip and then, figuring she might as well get something out of this miserable meeting, grabbed the bottle and followed suit. She wiped her mouth on the sleeve of her robe.

Not bad.

At least he had good taste in some things.

Without waiting to be invited, he prodded Rosy Cheeks over and took a seat on her futon. The ugly dog quivered as she gave him a thorough sniffing. When he'd passed the test, she allowed Rick to grip her around the middle and prop her in his lap. Little wheezes of pleasure issued from her nose as he gave her plump belly a vigorous rubbing.

Traitor. Cynthia scowled at her usually faithful companion. No more Oreos for her.

Rick's gaze roved about the compact kitchen and then around to the only two interior doors in her place, both open. One door led to her closet, overflowing with clothing, linens, books and other hodgepodge personal property. The other door led to her small bathroom, a cramped affair that—because of the positioning of the toilet—required the door to be open while one did one's business. One of the main reasons Cynthia didn't often entertain here at home.

"This a studio apartment?" Rick asked.

She nodded.

"This your bed?"

Again she took a swig of beer and nodded. He ran a hand over the mattress and then stared at her with a speculative eye. She didn't like his disapproving expression and could only imagine what was going through his mind. Clearly he considered her to be one of Graham's goodtime girls. And though nothing could have been farther from the truth, she squirmed under his scrutiny. She wished he would get off her bed and go home.

"You inherited the mansion."

She froze, not knowing how to respond. His boldness demanded an equal attitude, but he'd caught her off guard. "Uh, yes."

"That makes you rich."

A scowl marred her face as she wondered just where he was going with this. "I don't really see what business this is of yours."

"My family has always been my business."

"If that's true, where the hell have you been for the past two years?"

A curious mix of remorse and defensiveness flashed in his eyes. "I've been busy."

"Busy judging me."

"In my lifetime I've met my share of people like you."

"Since you seem to know so much about me already, you may as well leave."

"So soon? But Cyn, I just got here." His heavy boots thudded as he dropped his feet atop her spool coffee table. With a nod at her wicker chair he said, "Sit down. Take a load off. We have a lot of catching up to do."

Cynthia watched his Adam's apple bob as he took a long pull on his bottle, and decided that he was probably not going to leave any time soon. His lips made a smacking sound as he broke suction. Briefly she contemplated calling 911, but figured having her ex-fiancé's brother sitting on her futon and drinking a beer was probably not at the top of Seattle's finest's "emergency to-do" list.

She squinted long and hard at him and was irked to notice that he squinted back.

How this thug had made it through med school was beyond her ability to fathom. She wouldn't let this quack work on her car, let alone her body. However, deciding that it was probably easier to join him than to beat him, Cynthia dropped sullenly into her wicker rocker and drew her afghan up over her shoulders.

"So you think you know me."

He pointed at her with his bottle. "Oh, yeah. I know you. *You* wanna know about you? I'll tell you about you." Making himself at home, he slung his elbows up over the back of her couch and regarded her. "You are an opportunist."

"Oh. Um-hmm. Right." Cynthia took a swig of her own beer.

"Ah. So you agree with me."

"Do I have any choice?"

"No."

She bunched her shoulders to show that his opinion of her mattered not one whit. "You want to know about you?"

"No."

"Tough. I'm going to tell you anyway. You are a judgmental jackass."

"Oh. Um-hmm. Right."

For the first time since he'd arrived, they shared a brief grin. Very brief. When she noticed he was smiling, she sobered. He immediately followed suit. They resumed squinting at each other.

"You are a gold digger." Rick took another slug of beer.

"You are a sanctimonious slime." She did, too.

"You are only in this for the money."

"You are a holier-than-thou jerk."

He leaned forward and pointed an accusatory finger at her. "You take advantage of old people."

She pointed back. "You talk about things you know nothing about."

"At least I don't pretend I'm something I'm not."

"At least I don't pretend to know things I don't!"

They stared each other down even as they lifted their bottles and took another gulp of beer. Cynthia was beginning to feel pleasantly relaxed. Had to be the beer. She never indulged, so a single bottle usually had her cheeks warm and her mood elevated.

"So. You're marrying my brother."

Cynthia hesitated. Her failing relationship with Graham was none of his business. And since they hadn't announced their breakup to his parents yet, she decided to play her cards close to her chest. "Yes."

"Why?"

Her gaze met his and clashed defiantly. "Because—" She peeled the label off her bottle and crumpled it in her fist and tried to remember why she'd originally agreed to marry Graham. "Because I love him, of course."

"Love. Well, now. Isn't that…nice."

A slow fury began to burn in her belly, roiling upward and heating her cheeks. Who the hell did this guy think he was? *The arrogance! The audacity! The unmitigated gall!*

She itched to spring from her chair and slap that stupid stubble off his unshaven jaw. Her relationship with his brother was private! How dare he insinuate that this was not a love match, because it *was*. Once. A long time ago. Before Graham began to stray.

She was tempted to call Graham and cancel her cancellation. To marry Graham, just to spite his odious brother.

Then again, a lifetime with Graham would be her punishment, not Rick's.

As if he could read her thoughts, he smirked and—never breaking eye contact—opened his mouth, and his unapologetic belch had her jaw dropping in wonder. And this cretin thought *she* was the lowlife? She could take lessons from him. Again she wondered how the delicate Katherine could have spawned one of Satan's lower-class minions.

Completely grossed out, she simply stared at him as his head dropped back and he sprawled over her couch like a lion sunning on the tundra. He exuded the same lazy, yet untamed quality, which was both compelling and dangerous.

"I imagine you'll be moving out of here and up to the hill real soon."

"I haven't had time to give it much thought."

"Sure." Skepticism curled his lip.

Cynthia drained her bottle, then slammed it down on the spool. Rosy Cheeks looked up and woofed. "Are you always this pleasant?"

Lower teeth protruding, Rosy Cheeks eyed the man who was so proficient at a back rub.

"No." He grinned. "Sometimes I'm obnoxious."

Unable to stop it, she felt a grin graze her lips. She pulled it under control and asked, "What do you want from me?"

After a languid inspection, he said, "The pleasure of your company, tomorrow night at dinner."

"You want me to have dinner with you?"

"No. But my mother does. Be at their place at seven sharp, as she wants to be in bed by nine."

"I might have to work." She knew she didn't have an evening shift or class tomorrow, but she hated the way he took her acquiescence for granted.

He lifted a brow. "You work?"

"Of course I work," she snapped. "How do you think I support myself?"

The brow rose higher.

"You can go now." Cynthia threw off her afghan, leaped to the door and yanked it open in a most dramatic fashion. "Our little 'get acquainted' party is over."

"Awww." He made no move to leave. "Just as the ball was starting to roll."

"Speaking of rolling, you've got to, so bye-bye."

Leather squeaking, Rick dragged his feet off the spool and let them thud on the floor. Rosy Cheeks whimpered soulfully at his fond pat on the head.

Snagging his helmet off the futon, he ambled over to

where she stood by the door. Gooseflesh roared down her spine as he turned to face her, invading her personal space with his big old cretin self. He smelled like leather and motorcycle fumes and beer and something very male and not at all unpleasant. Directly in her line of vision, his chest rose and fell, stretching some ridiculous heavy metal band logo over his buffed-out pecs, and she wished he'd move into the hallway. His low voice and warm breath were unnerving.

From an upstairs apartment several students from the university could be heard cranking the stereo and spilling out into the hallway. Old Mrs. Allen shouted at them to shut the hell up, but as usual, they paid her no heed. A draft chilled the hallway and Cynthia wished she'd left her afghan wrapped around her shoulders. The cool air didn't seem to faze Rick, but then he was still glowing from the bowels of hell, she supposed, having just come from there to act as her own personal demon.

He brought his nose uncomfortably close to hers, and his face nearly went out of focus. Cynthia *hated* to have her space invaded. Especially by strangers. It made her antsy. Nervous. Wondering if she had something in her teeth, or the corners of her eyes. She looked up at him and attempted to exude some self-confidence.

Lordy, he had scary eyes.

"When will we know if you can make it to dinner?"

"I'll call your mother tomorrow."

"Okay. I'll tell her." He stood, not moving a muscle as he focused on her eyes, then her nose and then on down to her mouth. "Thanks for letting me drop in on you."

"You're not welcome. Don't try it again."

His lips quirked in amusement and appreciation flashed in his eyes. Reaching out, he gripped her upper arm and drew her even closer. "Good night, Cyn. It has been very…invigorating."

Before she could stop him, he settled his mouth over hers for a quick kiss and disappeared before she could react.

> *Hap-hap-hap-hap-hap-hap-happy birrr-rrrr-th-day!*
> *Hap-hap-hap-hap-hap-hap-happy birrr-rrrr-th-day!*
> *Hap-hap-hap-hap-hap-hap-happy birrr-rrrr-th-day!*
> *Hap-py birrr-rrrr-th-day!*
> *Oh, we know it is your birthday,*
> *You're looking kind of old,*
> *So have some cake and ice cream,*
> *Before you start to mold! Hey!*
>
> *Ohhhhhhh, hap-hap-hap-hap-hap...*

The next day—a crisp, sunny Saturday—found Cynthia wielding fluffy, felt-tipped drumsticks and banging away on the giant bass drum that hung suspended by a strap from her chest. With reluctance born of humiliation, she belted out the second verse of the obnoxious birthday song with her teenaged co-workers.

Yeah, yep, yeah. Mmm-hmm.

Just another delightful afternoon at Pudgie's Old-Fashioned Ice Cream Parlor.

The discordant caterwauling had her grimacing and she looked to the clock on the wall to calculate the hours left until quitting time. Oh, how she longed for her position with Alfred. At least this Pudgie's thing was temporary. For two months now, she'd endured this job in order to make ends meet after Alfred's health had taken a turn for the worse. And since she'd pondered her windfall all night long but still didn't know what to do about it, she'd forced herself to get up and come to work today. For the time being, she had no choice if she wanted to remain in school and off the streets.

Pudgie's was a remodeled firehouse, complete with a fire pole between floors and a fire-truck-cum-booth for the lucky birthday boy or girl. The employees—herself included—wore bright red fire hats, suspenders and rubber boots as part of their uniform. Fire-fighting memorabilia adorned every wall, and vintage uniforms and ladders and other sundry equipment cluttered every nook and cranny. Every fifteen minutes, a screen would drop from the ceiling and a cartoon featuring Freddy the Fireman would give the youngsters a spiel on fire safety.

The room in back was the arcade room and a gaggle of kids worked on their hearing loss as they crashed virtual race cars and chased after ninjas. Out front, one whole wall was filled with toys and candies and video games for sale. A huge oak bar salvaged from an 1800s saloon in downtown Seattle made up the counter, which was equipped with enough hoses and spray guns and seltzer bottles and flavorings for a literal month of sundaes.

As they rolled into verse three of the birthday song, Cynthia dodged a hot-dog bun, a fistful of fries and some crumpled napkins as the prepubescent patrons catcalled and jeered and made clear their opinion of the crew's dubious talent.

"Hey! You kids knock that off!" With a fierce scowl, Trent—the restaurant's manager—tried to control the aggressive birthday party. Clearly lacking proper parental supervision, the kids ran amok, and it seemed it was all Trent could do to keep from crowning several little monkeys with his tambourine.

Bored out of her gourd, Tiffany, the gum-chewing single mother and Britney Spears wanna-be, tapped at her triangle as she stared out the window.

Josh, the shy math whiz, puffed on his tuba and stared at Tiffany.

"Trent, I don't think they want us to sing anymore," Cynthia shouted over the hullabaloo.

The town idiot could see it was true, but Trent took his managerial position seriously, as he still owed his dad a bundle for his tricked-out Chevy. No truck payment equaled no football and, as his high school's star quarterback, no football wasn't an option. With Trent, rules were rules.

He punched his tambourine and glowered at her. "*I* say when we're done."

A half-eaten weenie rebounded off Trent's perfect coif.

"We're done." With that, he stalked off, leaving Cynthia and the others fizzling off at the end of verse three.

"Thank you." Cynthia nodded and smiled at the boisterous brats who bounced in the booth, and pulled Josh and Tiffany back to the ice-cream counter to begin working on the party's multitude of sundae orders.

"So." Tiffany paused to blow a bubble after they'd toiled for a while. "Cyn. Before the birthday song, you were telling us about the funeral and you just got to the part about your fiancé's phat, stupid brother. He sounds really bad. And cute."

Cute? Tiffany got *cute* out of her disparaging description? And her studies in teenage vernacular told her that Tiffany had just bestowed several of the highest compliments on Rick. Cynthia rolled her eyes. Well, that figured. Rick was just Tiffany's type. Wild. Reckless. The family's black sheep.

"I guess. If you like that sort."

The teen made silly smooching noises. "Um. I do."

"Isn't that why you got into trouble in the first place? You always pick the wrong guys?"

"I guess. But I'm pickier, now that I'm a mom."

"Which explains why you're all moony over Trent, when Josh—who is working his way through college and

has the potential to be the next Bill Gates, I might add—
is mad about you, *and* your baby.''

"But Trent is so cute."

"Josh is cute, too."

They looked up in time to see poor Josh slip on a blob
of ketchup and lose his tray of sundaes. The kids howled
with laughter and shouted for an encore.

"Trent is saving for a tattoo."

"Tiffany. Don't fall for the wrong guy."

"Like you did?"

"Like I did. But—" Cynthia sighed "—I broke up with
him."

"You *did? Why? You did?* But he's, like, loaded!"

"Wandering eye."

"Squid."

As Cynthia scooped the ice cream into dishes, Tiffany
fashioned faces of Gummi Bears and hats from waffle
cones. Trent jumped behind the counter to slap on the
whipped-cream hair, toss on the sprinkles, drizzle chocolate and flirt outrageously with Tiffany. As each order was
ready, he'd hammer on the bell to summon Josh, who ran
back and forth risking life and limb to deliver the rest of
the clown sundaes to the kids.

Cynthia couldn't believe she'd been confiding in the air-
headed Tiffany, but since she'd moved to Seattle she
hadn't really had the time or opportunity to make a lot of
girlfriends, and she needed to work this whole inheritance
thing out, aloud. Rosy Cheeks was not very good at feed-
back, and she could hardly call Katherine or Harrison for
advice.

At only twenty-four, she already felt as if she was the
girl's mother, but at least the kid was human.

Sort of.

Tiffany tossed her blond and neon-pink-tipped hair over
her shoulder and with long black nails peeled her wad of

gum off the spike that protruded from her tongue. "So you broke up with old stuffy boy. Whatever. You gonna go for his brother? What's his name?"

"Rick. Are you nuts?"

"Why not? I would. He sounds good."

"What's good?"

"Well, he sounds like…a free radical, you know? Like, his thing is not about being tense. Plus his style is—" Tiffany blew a bubble and pointed at a man approaching the counter "—you know, like his."

Cynthia glanced up.

"Fly," Tiffany breathed, and scooped a spoonful of sprinkles onto the floor.

"Rick," Cynthia gritted out from between tightly pursed lips. Blood boiling, she clutched the hot fudge gun. What was *he* doing here?

"Cyn." His gaze shot to her head. "Nice hat."

Chapter Three

"What are *you* doing here?"

"Charming. Do you welcome all of your customers this way?"

"Only the reptilian ones."

Wide-eyed, Tiffany stared back and forth between the two of them, her gaze lingering on Rick with thinly veiled appreciation. Josh was now attempting to quell the pandemonium coming from the juvenile delinquents, who claimed that they didn't want clown sundaes, they wanted Spiderman sundaes, and that clown sundaes were for babies.

Trent was behind him threatening to bash some birthday heads.

"Tiffany, isn't it time for you to go home? You're on overtime as it is." Cynthia cast a bright smile at the child who was suddenly staring at her with an "areyou*nuts?*" expression. Why, oh why had she told the girl that she'd broken off her engagement with Graham? Surely she'd blab and the jig would be up.

"You gotta be kidding! It's a *zoo* in here."

"This little group? Nah. They've got their orders. We're done." Hands flapping, Cynthia tossed out some carefree laughter and forced some little *pbbshht* sounds between her lips to prove that the riot over in the corner was no big deal. "Josh and Trent have everything under control and I can handle the counter. Go. Now. Really."

Rick winked at the young girl. "Is she always this bossy?"

Tiffany grinned. "Yeah."

"Here." Cynthia dug deep in her pockets. She regularly sent Tiffany home with her Saturday tips, as the girl never seemed to have enough money for life's little luxuries. Like food for her baby. As she tucked the smallish wad into the girl's hands, she could feel Rick's scrutiny. No doubt he figured they were making some kind of illegal drug deal. A glance at Tiffany's obscenely low hip-hugging jeans and her multipierced and bejeweled navel made her think that she would be under the same impression if she didn't know better. "Go on, now."

"But I still think I should stay and help you guys...."

"Trent won't mind. I can handle it. Go."

"Okay. If you're sure."

"I'm sure."

Tiffany removed her fire hat and hung it on its peg, punched her card in the time clock and with a last, lingering look at Rick, left.

Arms crossed at his chest, Rick leaned against the bar and studied Cynthia. "Why the bum's rush?"

"She has a baby at home. So. Why are you here?"

"I wanted a little lunch. Is that a crime?"

"And you came here of all places. What a coincidence." Cynthia tossed the ice cream scoops into buckets of water and began to mop down the floor behind the stainless-steel prep area. He didn't believe that she actually had a job, and so he'd had to come and see for himself. Jerk.

"My reasons for being here are not all selfish. I also came on behalf of my mother, who is still wondering whether you're plan—"

"Oh, fiddlesticks!" Cynthia dropped her mop and slapped her forehead with her palm, knocking her plastic fire helmet askew. "I forgot to call your mother about dinner tonight."

The horrendous rumble of several unmufflered diesel engines in the parking lot obscured her lame explanation. It was a lucky thing, as he wasn't in the mood to listen to a pack of lies. Arms gesticulating wildly, she ranted, counting off a litany of excuses on her slender fingers while two chartered buses jockeyed about the parking lot, gears a-grinding. As her diatribe wound down, the buses settled into a pair of minuscule slots just outside the picture window and came to a halt with a long, steamy hiss.

Rick watched Cynthia's eyes widen in alarm as, behind him, the doors blew open and the entire U. Dub football team—including cheerleaders, coaches and friends—carried a player in on their shoulders, shouting, catcalling and laughing.

"Two tables for thirty! We got a birthday here!" one barrel-chested, barrel-necked, barrelhead shouted into his megaphone, and the young men hooted and hollered and jostled and tossed their 250-pound birthday boy at the ceiling as if he were a rag doll.

Jaws slack, Josh and Trent turned their backs on the younger kids to stare. The room seemed to shrink considerably as the burly boys dragged their tables and chairs into the middle of the room and made themselves at home. One obvious Pudgie's regular knew where the siren switch was at the end of the bar and the ensuing wail was likely splitting ears well into the next county.

"Hey, babe!" The barrelhead with the megaphone jumped off the table and rushed to Cynthia. "You are one dishy fireman!" Grabbing her around the waist, he lifted her off the floor. After a couple spins that had her clutching her fire hat and pounding his chest, he set her down and continued his amplified shouting. He also continued holding her around the waist. *"We want the birthday song! The birthday song! Birthday song!"*

The barrelhead's hands roved over Cynthia's hips and bottom, causing Rick's blood pressure to spike just a tad. Not that he cared who she chose to party with, of course. It was the principle of the thing, he told himself. No waitress should be subjected to such familiar contact. Not even a con-artist waitress, biding her time until she could abscond with the family fortune.

"Birthday song! Birthday song! Birthday song!"

Cynthia slapped the barrelhead's hands as the team joined him in his chant. The siren wailed. The chandeliers swayed. The windows rattled. The juvenile delinquents demanded Spiderman sundaes.

Rick found himself gaping with wonder. Was it like this every Saturday? If so, how was the place still standing? Only a saint would put up with this crap for very long. In third-world countries he'd lived among gorillas with more dining decorum. A sudden, unbidden burst of admiration for Cynthia struck him, but he chased it away with the truth. This was a temporary gig, meant to impress his family with her solid work ethic.

Trent finally snapped-to and, with Josh hot on his heels, ran to the counter and began barking orders.

"Cynthia! Josh! Tiffany! Grab your instruments. They're not gonna shut up till we sing."

Cynthia and Josh squinted at him, lip-reading over the din.

"Tiffany went home!" Cynthia mouthed, and she and Josh donned their instruments.

"*What?*" Veins bulging, beads of sweat popping, face flushing, Trent looked ready to explode. "*Who* the *hell* told her she could *do that?*"

Wielding the fluffy drumstick, Cynthia pulled her shoulders back and pointed at her Napoleonic boss. "I did. It was past her quitting time and she needed to feed her baby."

Rick stroked his bottom lip with his thumb. Huh. Seemed she told the truth now and then. And he had to admire the way she was standing up to jerky jock.

"And just *who* do you *think* is gonna *play* the *triangle?*"

Cynthia darted a disgusted glance at the ceiling. "We'll do without."

Fortunately there was too much noise to hear the string of expletives that escaped young Trent's lips. "No *way!*" he screamed. "The *rules* state that *all* instruments *must* be played during the *Happy* Birthday song! Make your boyfriend there do it."

"He's not my—"

"*Just do it!*" Eyes bulging, Trent tossed the triangle and a fire hat at Rick and shouted, "On three!"

Fielding the hat before it hit the floor, Rick popped it on his head and stared at the triangle in his hand. They wanted him to play this stupid thing? And sing? *Now?*

The football team climbed up onto the tables, twirling the birthday boy overhead. "*Birthday song! Birthday song! Birthday song!*"

"One! Two! *Three!*"

Rick shrugged and began to beat his triangle. What the heck. He had nothing better to do with his Saturday.

Cynthia could feel the sweat trickling between her shoulder blades as she slung yet another sundae dish down the bar to Rick for the toppings. Apparently there was a puny heart somewhere in that burly chest, she thought with grudging appreciation. As a doctor, he probably wanted to stave off Trent's inevitable cardiac arrest. The poor kid was fairly catatonic with panic.

Trent slammed the order bell. "Gimme a Volcanic Eruption for a dozen, sixteen Belly Busters, one without nuts, eight Pudgie's Pork-Outs and nine Bahama Mama Banana Splits—two without pineapple sauce—and four diet sodas. How we coming on the Spiderman sundaes?"

He didn't wait around to find out. The birthday boy's head had just cracked a ceiling tile.

"Son of a *gun!*" Rick exploded, and stuck his thumb in his mouth. "This sucker is *hot!*"

Cynthia glanced up and grinned. The hot fudge gun liked to sputter and pop when the compressor pumped too much air into the lines. He looked just like a cowboy out of ammo as he stood hunched over his lopsided sundae. Muttering under his breath, he aimed the gun between his eyes and glowered down the barrel.

"Don't!" Cynthia dropped her scoop and rushed to his side. "That's a good way to blister your face."

"I didn't know you cared."

"I don't, but right now you're all we've got." She pried the gun from his hands and demonstrated. "Here. Like this."

Expertly she topped the sundae and pushed it on a tray for Josh. Rick gave his head a cocky little nod and grabbed the gun back.

"Got it." It seemed he was showing off as he pointed the gun at the scoop of ice cream and blew it out of the bowl and onto the floor.

"You killed it," she deadpanned.

"For crying in the *night,*" he shouted, and beat the gun

on the countertop. "Medical school was easier than this stupid job!"

"I know. But don't take it out on the poor hot fudge gun. If you break it, we're really up a creek."

"Oh, and we're not now?" he grumbled with a glance at the free-for-all going on in the dining room.

"You think this is bad, you should have been here over Labor Day End of Summer Blowout."

She handed him the gun, and this time closed her hands over his. She could tell by the way it rested in his palm that he was pulling up and back on the trigger, instead of straight back. Classic new-guy mistake. She'd done it herself at first, until she'd got the hang of it.

"See?" Cynthia leaned against his arm and, helping him point at an empty bowl, gently guided his trigger finger straight back. He nodded as the hot fudge dispensed an expert stream. "Good," she murmured. "Um-hum. Like that."

His face awash with concentration, he became suddenly oblivious to the chaos that roiled out front. An excellent trait in a doctor, she suspected. Must be the earthquakes he'd survived these past years. Good training for Pudgie's. Slowly she let go of his hands and backed away. The gun sputtered.

"No, no, no. Here." She slipped under his arms and stood between him and the bowl. Taking his hands into hers once again, she helped him load a bowl. "Good. Now you've got it."

He grunted as the gun popped.

"Don't worry. It does that all the time. The tip is probably a little bit clogged." She leaned back against his chest and glanced up at him with a reassuring smile.

"Hey!" Trent hollered as he rushed up to the counter and gave the order bell a thrashing. "We don't have time for you guys to make out now! You can do that stuff on your own time!''

Cynthia stiffened, mortified. *Make out?*

Rick, on the other hand, grinned.

''Aww,'' he protested, ''this job is a real drag if ya' can't even fool around now and then.''

He closed his arms around Cynthia's waist and growled into her neck. She was sure her suddenly scalding flesh was burning his roving lips. He smacked and slurped and rocked her to and fro. Completely helpless in his steely grasp, she found herself emitting some giggly squeaks of horror at the absurdity. That, and the fact that the stubble at his chin was tickling her neck.

Trent gave the bell another menacing spanking and then stalked off to deliver the five-gallon Volcanic Eruption. As unobtrusively as possible, Josh swept up little piles of corkboard ceiling tile.

Ducking under Rick's arm, Cynthia moved back to her station and dared not look him in the eye, for fear she'd laugh. As much as she hated to admit it, Rick Wingate was a pretty funny guy. When he wanted to be.

Which, she suspected, wasn't often.

Metal legs thundered over linoleum as Rick dragged tables and chairs back into their original spots. Cynthia simply couldn't believe he was still there. What a glutton for punishment. Either that, or he was hoping to catch her with her hands in Pudgie's till.

The din Rick created suddenly stopped and she watched as he—with a loud yawn—pushed his thumbs into his lower back and arched and stretched.

''Uh-oh.'' He exhaled, his eyes fixed in the direction of the clock.

''What uh-oh?'' With a splash Cynthia tossed her cloth

into the pail of ammonia water. She propped her hands on a sticky tabletop and peered at him.

"I was supposed to call Mom two hours ago, so she could inform the cook of your decision."

Exhausted and disheveled, she glanced up at the clock and groaned. Five o'clock. Time for the next shift to take over. The kiddy party and the football team had come and gone, and since then they'd had a record number of birthdays. Rick had become quite adept at playing the triangle with finesse and could belt out the birthday song with the best of them.

He spun a chair around backward and, straddling it, dropped into its seat. Chin resting on the back, he asked, "Have you decided to come over for dinner tonight?"

"That depends."

"On what?"

"On whether or not you'll be there."

Curiosity lifted his brow a notch. "I was planning on eating, yes."

"Then I will have to send my regrets."

"Oh. So that's how it is. I hit a little too close to the truth about Alfred's will last night and so now you're avoiding me. Hey, I extended an olive branch today. The least you could do is meet me halfway." He angled his head.

Cynthia snorted. She could sense him still watching her as she turned her back and begin fussing with an empty chrome napkin dispenser. Yes, it was true. He'd been Pudgie's salvation today. But that didn't mean she had to go out of her way to spend time in his company.

There was something about him that made her edgy.

Squirrelly.

As if she needed to defend herself for something she hadn't even done. And even though he'd relaxed for a few minutes and played with her earlier—teasing Trent about being her boyfriend—she had the sneaking suspicion he'd taken the liberty because he thought she was fast and easy.

So, that being the case, she didn't feel all that bad about wanting to have dinner with Katherine and Harrison alone. They had things to discuss that had absolutely nothing to do with their snoopy older son. In the reflection of the plate-glass window she watched him stand and swing the chair under its table.

"Okay, then. So be it. In that case, I'll call Mom and tell her you'll be there by seven. I guess I'll have to find other ways to occupy my evening."

Rick pulled open the front door of his parents' house, rocked back on his heels and hooked his thumbs in the loops of his jeans. Through smirking lips he eyeballed Cynthia up and down and drawled, "Surprise. I lied."

Mouth tight, she huffed in disgust. "Somehow I knew you would."

"I know, I know. You'd never lie."

Cynthia glared.

"But you don't mind my hanging around. After all, it's not like you have anything to hide from me, right?"

Ignoring his question, she pushed past him and, shrugging out of her coat, tossed it at him with her free hand. "Here."

"Thanks." Her pluck amused him and he had to battle the laughter as he opened the front closet door, wadded up her coat and threw it inside.

Watching him, she emitted a little grunt of displeasure. And when he tried to wrest away the package she clutched, she jerked back and scowled.

"Has anyone ever told you you're an absolute animal?"

"Only on very special occasions."

"Spare me."

"Mom and Dad are in the family room."

Over the snippy tippity-tapping of her heels across the floor, he caught a snatch of her mutterings about finding civilization, and gave himself permission to laugh. She had moxie. He'd give her that much.

He set off after her as she rushed through the foyer. Smoothly she navigated the highly polished table—topped by a monstrous bouquet of fall flowers in a Ming vase—and moved under the arches, down the expansive hallway and into the family room, as if she'd lived there all her life.

In a conversation grouping of comfortable chairs, Katherine and Harrison were lounging in front of the fire, sipping brandy from gold-rimmed crystal snifters. Eyes crinkling, they patted the cushion of a nearby chair and beckoned Cynthia to join them.

"Rick, darlin', pour Cynthia here a drink, will you?" Katherine instructed as her son strode into the room behind Cynthia.

Cynthia eyed him haughtily, then smiled at Katherine. "No, nothing for me, thank you. I did bring something for you, however." She held out her large gift bag, all beribboned and overflowing with tissues.

"How sweet! You didn't have to do that, darlin'!"

"I know. I wanted to. I didn't know how to express my sympathy for your loss and so…"

Heavy silence suddenly reigned.

In the mirror over the wet bar Rick watched her gesture awkwardly to the bag. Seemed she hoped that its contents would make up for her inheriting the house out from under them, he guessed a tad churlishly. He grabbed a water from the wet bar's small refrigerator and, bottles tinkling, slammed the door.

Katherine sighed as Harrison placed an arm around his wife's shoulders. "Oh, thank you, honey. I think it will take us all a while to get beyond…you know…everything.

But it'll be all right. We're happy here in our little home, aren't we, hon?''

A hum rumbled from Harrison's throat as he moved his unlit pipe into the corner of his mouth and nodded. "Home is where the heart is."

Katherine sighed.

With long, delicate fingertips, Cynthia smoothed her skirt. "Yes. Well." Again there was a moment that a Sherman tank could have driven through. "Yes. Well." Desperate to relieve the tension, she donned a bright smile and nudged at the bag. "Go on. Open it."

A barely inquisitive Katherine shrugged and, reaching inside, murmured, "My, it's heavy!"

Harrison leaned forward for a better look as his wife withdrew an ornate birdhouse. In his Bing Crosby voice he marveled, "Ho now, will you look at that!"

"Isn't that just darlin'?" Katherine held the beautiful house up for all to see.

Her eyes sparkling, Cynthia pulled back the tissues that clung to the tiny wooden corbels and spindles and said demurely, "I made it myself."

"You *made* it!" Laboring beneath its weight, Katherine held the birdhouse out to Harrison, who set it in his lap. "How about that, dear? She made it."

"Mmm," Harrison droned around his pipe. "It's more than a birdhouse, wouldn't you say? More like a bird mansion." They all chuckled.

Water bottle in hand, Rick moved in to stand behind his mother to get a better look.

Cynthia *made* this thing? No way. He leaned a little closer. It was truly a work of art. He pressed the mouth of the bottle to his lips and became skeptical as he took in the amazing detail. When in the world would she have time—not to mention the shop and tools—to make something like this, if she were truly a student? And with that

nut-ball job of hers? His ears were still ringing from
Pudgie's melee.

How much baloney did she expect them to swallow?

"I've been working on it for several weeks because I
had to hand cut all of the fish-scale shingles and the posts
for the porch with my Dremal tool set. I thought it might
look nice in your garden."

Rick snorted.

Brows locked, Cynthia shot him an annoyed glance.
Head snapping away, she took a deep breath, then focused
one of her soft, beautiful smiles upon his father.

"I put some little furniture inside, but there is still plenty
of room for a nest. See the little weather vane on the cu-
pola? And the tiny front porch with the picket fence?"

"Seems too pretty to put outside," Katherine mused.

Cynthia's smile was shy at the compliment. "I don't
have a mother of my own to fuss over, but you two have
been so wonderful and are the closest thing to real parents—"

Rick wheezed and sputtered over the big gulp of water
he sucked down the wrong pipe.

Shoulders pulled back, Cynthia ignored his coughing fit,
simply lifting her voice to be heard above the commotion.
"I'm told my mother loved birds. And they say my dad
was a very creative guy. He used to build her wonderful
little houses. I still have one to remember them by, on top
of my refrigerator. That's where I got the idea to send for
the pattern from *Better Homes and Gardens* magazine."

"Are you all right, dear?" Katherine twisted to peer up
at her sputtering son.

"Yeah. I'll be fine." Rick wiped his eyes on his sleeves.
Oh, yeah. She was good.

Playing up his mother's gullibility with some cocka-
mamy bird story. Very clever. No dummy, this one.

"Darlin', I have the perfect spot to display your birdhouse! The ladies down at the ornithological society will just love it. I'll donate it on Monday!'' With the tinkle of a bell, Katherine summoned a member of the staff and summarily dispensed with the birdhouse over which Cynthia had so painstakingly labored this past month.

Leaning back against the wet bar, Rick studied the two women—Katherine, beaming, and Cynthia, crestfallen for just a moment as she realized that Katherine was not going to keep her gift.

With a stoic smile Cynthia rallied, and feigned excitement about Katherine's suggestion, but Rick could see the hurt was real.

A rogue pang of sympathy shot through him as he remembered similar thoughtless moments in his own youth. His mother's insensitive ways irked him still.

But he had to wonder why he was so bothered in this instance. After all, Cynthia was a liar and his mother, though sweet, was from another planet. Why should he worry about either of them?

But he did.

And worse still, he disgusted himself for admiring the way Cynthia had worked so hard today.

Arms over his head, Rick stretched and could feel the sore muscles in his neck and back. There were blisters on his hands from the hot fudge gun and his feet were killing him. He stifled a groan.

Pudgie's was hell.

He was completely exhausted, and he didn't have a pile of homework waiting for him later tonight. Josh had told him that Cynthia was in several of his language arts classes and that they had a test in one, first thing in the morning. Also, Josh had let on that she was always the professor's pet. Just as she'd been Alfred's.

With an imperceptible shake of his head, Rick tried to reconcile his suspicions with fact.

The con game just didn't add up at some points.

Yet.

As he finished off the rest of his water, he knew he needed to find out more about her. Watch every move she made, until he figured out what she and Graham were up to. From the strange, rattled expression on her face when he'd quizzed her last night about why she was marrying his brother, he'd gotten the funniest feeling it wasn't about love. There was some kind of unholy alliance going on between the two of them and it involved secrets.

Fine. Since he was between foreign medical assignments, a little mystery to keep him interested might be just the diversion he needed.

The Wingate dining room was a study in fine, upper-class, suburban living. The wainscoting was fashioned from cherry wood and, above that, the walls were covered by rich calfskin leather. Over the center of the table hung twin chandeliers loaded with tiny black Austrian crystals that sparkled by candlelight. A freshly cut bouquet of tropical flowers graced the center of the table, and the goblets each held a dash of hundred-year-old wine.

Two kitchen-staff persons unobtrusively slipped in and out of the lavish dining room, delivering gourmet fare to the foursome. The food smelled as if it had been divinely inspired and prepared, and each plate was a work of art.

When the main course—consisting of beef medallions in a subtle dark French wine sauce, and fresh garden vegetables spiced and grilled to perfection—was delivered, Cynthia could only bring herself to nibble.

Unfortunately, feeling as if she was being cross-examined by Graham's older brother, she couldn't swallow a bite of the lovely meal. It all sat in her mouth like so much cotton batting, making chewing an endless and miserable ordeal.

Rick, on the other hand, ate with gusto, wolfing down two plates of each serving and looking around for more. The cretin did not seem to care about the art of polite conversation and instead enjoyed pointing at her with his fork and pummeling her with questions as he chewed.

"So you're taking your time to earn your degree? What's the hang-up?"

Cynthia gave the corners of her mouth a delicate pat with her linen napkin. "Well, I—"

"Where did you say you came from again?"

"I—"

"Wait, hang on. Tell me one more time, just how did you meet my grandfather? He's the one that got you together with Graham, right? So tell us all, how did you end up snagging my brother? I mean, he's not exactly the marrying kind, if you get my drift."

Katherine cleared her throat, but Rick paid no heed to the polite warning as he warmed to his interrogation.

"And another thing, why are you studying so many foreign languages? Where do you plan on going from here? I mean, after all, it's not like you are planning to run off to another country anytime soon, are you? Especially without my brother. Are you and Graham always apart for such long periods of time? In fact, just where the hell is he, these days?"

"Good gracious!" Katherine finally intervened with an aghast giggle. "Rick, darlin', you're going to scare our sweet Cynthia half to death with all these personal questions."

The fork he so accusingly pointed at her wobbled with his shrug and Cynthia suspected scaring her was his agenda, as a small smile tugged at his chiseled lips.

"Sorry." He didn't sound a bit sorry, but he did fall silent, which was somehow even worse, as he did not remove his gaze from her, but simply probed with those deep, dark, all-knowing, all-seeing eyes. The quirk in his brow fairly screamed, *I'm on to you.*

A tiny flash of panic had her heart suddenly thrumming. Did he know she'd broken off her engagement to Graham? No. How could he? Unless he'd overheard them talking...

Cynthia looked away.

Forcing her gaze everywhere but on him, she took time to study the half-dozen oil paintings on the dining room's vast walls behind Rick's head. Art was a neutral subject. She would begin a one-on-one conversation with Katherine. Many of the beautiful paintings appeared to be originals. Surrounded by ornate gilt frames, they looked as if they should be hanging in a museum.

Cynthia indicated a Rubenesque woman holding a cherub in her lap. "That one's sweet. Who's the artist?"

Rick leaned forward. "You interested in priceless art?"

Afraid she'd cracked one of her rear molars in her fury, Cynthia exploded. "Oh, for the love of—!"

Luckily for all, the staff chose that moment to burst through the dining-room doors and begin clearing their plates. Seeming to sense the tension building between her son and future daughter-in-law, Katherine suggested that they all adjourn to the great room for slices of Death by Chocolate and conversation.

Cynthia glowered at Rick's irreverent grin and hoped that, in his case anyway, the dessert would live up to its name. She stood and fired her napkin to the seat of her chair. As she marched after Katherine and Harrison, she could sense Rick dogging her like a parole officer bucking for promotion.

"Would you please back *off*," she hissed.

Rick joined her on one of the two facing love seats, invading her space in a most annoying way.

"I will if you will."

Cynthia snorted at the double meaning behind his words.

He'd perched on the edge of the center cushion in such a way that he leaned heavily on her, his elbow settling into the crook of her arm and his thigh pressing hers from hip to knee. Cynthia tried to move away, but the chubby love seat's overstuffed arm left her with no place to go. She could feel the warmth radiating from his body and could smell the latte on his breath.

His grin was huge, in her face and most disconcerting.

For such a big guy, loaded down with muscle the way he was, it surprised Cynthia how comfortable he was to lean against. The flesh on his arms was smooth and soft, even though the muscle that lay beneath was bulging steel. In the chill of encroaching winter, and in far different circumstances, she might have enjoyed having him sitting so ridiculously close. And keeping her warm.

But not tonight.

That he suspected her of some heinous crime was obvious. And until he could get beyond that, she would do her best to steer clear. She set her latte on the end table and hiked her body closer to the arm of the couch.

Unfortunately, Rick followed, pinning her skirt under his thunderous, muscle-corded thigh. His smart-aleck grin broadened as she tried to tug it free.

Katherine and Harrison settled across from them on the matching love seat. Joining hands, they relaxed and smiled at each other with love in their eyes. The devotion between them was charming as Katherine leaned into her husband's sunken chest and sipped her coffee and listened to the merry crackling of the fire. Pipe smoke made a wreath of sorts around their heads, putting Cynthia in mind of a Norman Rockwell painting.

"They're cute, aren't they?" Rick murmured.

She gave her head a curt bob. They were cute. She envied them their enduring love. Too bad that kind of thing wasn't in the cards for her.

Oh, well.

She had a lot to be thankful for. Good friends, an education, a job—such as it was—a roof over her head and Rosy Cheeks. Slowly Cynthia relaxed back into her seat and ignored Rick's arm as he moved it up and over the back of their chair.

One of the kitchen staff served the dessert and then bid them good-night. From the mantel, a clock chimed the hour in low tones. The fire consumed an oak log with cheerful popping and hissing noises. Forks tinked against fine china as they ate in relative silence.

And eating was no small feat for Cynthia, being that Rick had her pinned into the corner of the small couch. She could barely move her arm and had to duck her head and maneuver her fork just so, to keep from missing her mouth.

Rick didn't seem to notice.

When at last Katherine set her barely touched plate on the coffee table, the silence was broken.

"I do believe I'm going to have to turn in a tad early this evening. Tomorrow is a big day." A sad smile graced her lips. "I'll be supervising the unpacking of many of our household goods, as we won't be moving up to the mansion on the hill, after all."

Humiliation stained Cynthia's cheeks. "I—I'm sorry."

"Oh, we know it's not your fault, Cynthia." Harrison's lighter snicked several times as he relit his pipe.

"No, no, of course not." Katherine slumped farther beneath her husband's armpit. "Truly, it's not your fault, darlin'."

"No indeed. My father was an unpredictable guy. We should have predicted that." Puffs of aromatic smoke curled into the air.

Katherine nodded listlessly. "Truth is, we didn't really want to move. We enjoy our cozy neighborhood. Although a certain number of the bourgeoisie have encroached lately, with their little SUVs and Club Med holidays… But Alfred couldn't have known that…."

"No. Dad couldn't have known that."

Cynthia squirmed and could feel Rick cock his head, interested in her every reaction.

"At any rate, the reason we invited you to come for dinner tonight," Harrison continued, "is that we wanted to talk to you about your inheritance. After giving the whole thing careful consideration, we think that Alfred was quite right to give you and Graham the house."

"Actually, Dad, he gave the house to Cynthia," Rick piped up.

"Yes, yes, whatever." Katherine threw an arm up over her eyes and took several cleansing breaths as she came to terms with the truth. "You know, I've been thinking, Cynthia darling. There are many advantages to your inheriting the house. It's time that Graham finally… er…settled down. I'm hoping that your ownership of the family homestead will be the nudge he needs to send him down the aisle as soon as possible."

Harrison's chuckle rumbled.

Rick snorted.

Cynthia opened her mouth to protest. "Oh, no—"

Katherine interrupted. "And speaking of weddings—" she leveled her gaze at Cynthia and smiled "—perhaps we should begin discussing yours and Graham's."

"Oh, no—"

Eyes huge behind his thick glasses, Harrison peered at his wife. "Sweetheart, is that a spark I see in your eye?"

Becoming somewhat animated, Katherine pushed herself nearly upright, her gaze floating about. "Well…come to think of it, this very room would be the perfect place to hold a wedding. In fact, it might be something to look forward to, in these rather…grief-stricken days.''

Cynthia knew the grief had as much to do with losing the estate house as with losing Alfred. ''Oh?'' she croaked. ''But what about Graham? Surely we should consult him—''

Katherine chuckled. ''If we consult him, nothing will ever get done. Besides, there is no real reason to wait. Isn't that right, Harrison? In fact—'' She sat up a little straighter, no longer needing Harrison's support. ''Why don't we begin immediately and aim for the twenty-third, as everyone is always home for the holidays.''

''The…holidays?'' Cynthia's blood ran cold. Unless she was referring to the Fourth of July, Christmas was only three weeks away.

''I can just see it now.'' Hands to cheeks, Katherine watched the movie that was now rolling in her mind. ''The doves. The swans in the reflecting pool. The horse-drawn carriage. We can light the fountain with the holiday colors. Why, my land! It will be something out of a fairy tale.'' The speed and pitch of her voice increased with her verve. ''I'm thinking a small, intimate affair for family and a few close friends. Then we can all head over to Alfred's—I mean,'' she corrected, embarrassed, ''*your* place for the much larger, more inclusive reception. We'll invite everyone we know.''

''That's the spirit.'' Harrison hummed his approval.

Horrified, Cynthia excused herself, disentangled her body from Rick's and bolted from the room.

Chapter Four

Icy water sluiced over Cynthia's wrists as she stood before the mirror in the powder room and surveyed her reflection. It was astonishing to see such a calm exterior staring back at her, for inside, she was a swirling mass of panic and anxiety.

Katherine was beginning to plan her wedding to Graham!

Doves and swans and carriage rides! Oh, my!

Her throat grew thick and her head light. She could hear the jungle beat of her heart over the rushing water and feared she was about to faint dead away where, most certainly, the odious Dr. Rick would discover her draped over the toilet.

No.

She had to pull herself together. Cupping her hands beneath the flow, she filled them with water, splashed her face and resolved to buck up. The fluffy, monogrammed towel felt good pressed to her flushed cheeks, and she forced herself to breathe more slowly.

She had to think.

There was no way she could let Katherine actually begin planning this charade. Before she knew it, she and Harrison would spend a fortune on a nonexistent wedding, giving them even more fodder for disowning her. Her heart threatened to choke her as it crowded into her throat.

She had to get hold of Graham.

Now.

If only she'd thought to pin him down for a contact number before he left for Boston. Last night, after Rick left, she'd repeatedly dialed Graham's cell phone, only to have the automated operator come on and tell her, "The cellular customer you wish to contact is out of the area."

That much she knew.

Graham had either turned off his private phone and was using the company cell, or he was doing business from his hotel room via Internet conferencing. Either way, she was out of luck until Monday when she could call his office for the various numbers.

Cynthia exhaled in a long, leaky hiss. How on earth had she let him get away without an emergency phone number? What a major-league boob.

Although, on her behalf, she had been just the tiniest little bit distracted before he'd packed and departed. Slowly she folded the towel and hung it back on its rack. Unfortunately, asking Harrison for the number would seem very strange. After all, why wouldn't an ardent bride have been on the phone with her fiancé constantly since the moment he'd left? She gave the faucet's porcelain knob a savage twist—wishing it were Graham's head—and wondered if he'd thought to give his parents his number.

Common sense told her that if he had, she might find it in Harrison's office, opposite the bathroom. Yes. *That was it.* She'd get the number without anyone being the wiser.

With a gentle creak the door swung open and she looked

both ways before stepping into the empty hall. Sounds of lively chitchat reached her from the great room, where she'd left the family for too long already.

She glanced at her watch.

Okay…perhaps, if she hurried, she could slip into the office and rummage through Harrison's Rolodex and other sundry phone lists, grab the number and make it back without arousing suspicion. With any luck she'd be on the phone giving Graham a piece of her mind that very evening.

That is, if she had a piece left to give.

Heart beating like a jackhammer, Cynthia tiptoed across the hall and into Harrison's office. Gooseflesh roared down her appendages and her vision began to fade to black from the fear of being discovered. Clearly she didn't possess Miss Marple's gutsy sleuthing chops. Flopping forward, she clutched her ankles to forestall the hyperventilation that threatened. Though she knew the staff had been excused for the evening, she peered between her knees for good measure.

So far, so good.

She sucked in some precious oxygen and slowly stood.

A lone lamp sent a shaft of light across the desk, lighting Harrison's giant Rolodex as if it were the Holy Grail. Bingo!

She hesitated.

After all, this *was* Harrison's private domain.

Then again, so what? This was an emergency.

Rushing to the desk, she grabbed hold of the Rolodex's knob and gave it an impatient spin. Unfortunately her fervor was more than the overloaded phone directory could bear and cards flew, as if jet-propelled, everywhere.

"Dam*nation!*" Hands to her face, she froze and listened.

Okay. They were still talking. Good, good.

Dropping to her hands and knees, Cynthia crawled about, frantically gathering the cards and trying to alphabetize them before someone began to wonder what kind of ptomaine poisoning was keeping her in the bathroom so long.

"*H-I-J-K*—uh, *N,* no, uh… Norton, Naughton would be uh…first…*ABCDEFG*—" She sang the alphabet song under her breath as she struggled to put the cards in order. "'Next time, won't you sing with me?'" Beads of sweat broke out on her brow. This was going to take forever. She pawed through the pile, looking for Graham's number. "Winston, Williams, Winters…nnnnno. Okay, maybe it's under *G.*"

Rick's suspicions grew with every second that ticked past on the mantel clock. She'd been gone plenty long enough to powder her nose and take care of whatever other personal functions needed attention. So, where the Sam Hill was she? And what was she up to? He'd tuned out his mother's excited plans and was at a loss when she addressed him.

"—could stand in for Graham until he gets here, right before the wedding. That way, we wouldn't be delayed in any serious manner with the fittings, rehearsals and other traditional duties. What do you think, Rick, darling? Rick? Darling?"

"I'm sorry, Mom. I was drifting. Listen, would you excuse me for just a moment? I promise I'll be right back."

"Of course, dear."

She waved him away and the animated ideas and questions she pelted poor Harrison with grew dim as Rick ambled from the great room and into the hall. Cynthia had used the rest room as an excuse for her escape, but he doubted he'd find her there after all this time.

Unless she was sick. This, he decided, would be the

excuse he'd offer for checking up on her, being that he was a doctor.

Moving soundlessly down the corridor, he listened. From inside the house came the murmurs of his parents' voices. From outside, a neighbor's car door slammed and an engine purred to life. Off in the distance several dogs barked. It was quiet for a Saturday night.

Rick paused and strained to hear, just outside the door of the nearest bathroom. Not a creature was stirring. Then again...

He inched across the hall and stopped just short of his father's office. Some second sense had him freeze. The quiet shuffle of papers sounded and a drawer slid open, then closed. More shuffling, and then the clicking sounds of a Rolodex being cranked into position.

And then the low tones of someone singing.

The *alphabet song?*

Now, who, other than Cynthia, would be in his father's office at this time of night? The staff had been excused and it was just the four of them in the house. He inched to the door and peered through the crack.

Inexplicably his heart sank.

Just as he'd suspected.

Cynthia was rummaging through his father's personal effects. She was the impostor he'd thought her to be, after all.

"Hi." The word shot out of his mouth in a clipped, derisive fashion.

She snapped up, startled. Guilty.

"Hi."

He could see the wheels turning in her pretty head as she hastily made up an excuse for snooping through his father's desk.

"I...I...was looking for a breath mint." She scooped

a pile of Rolodex cards into a desk drawer and beamed at him.

"A breath mint? Why bother? Your fiancé is away. None of us care if you—" his lips curled in derision as he moved beyond the door and into the office proper "—reek."

At his approach, she stepped around to the front of the desk, trying to appear collected, but breathing with a bit of difficulty. Rick had to give her credit for bravery. That, and the ability to think on her feet. *A breath mint.* Wasn't the most original excuse, but at least she was giving it the good old college try.

She swallowed. "I just thought that after all that coffee…"

"Oh, come on. We're all family here. Accepting. Loving." With a slow, lazy gait, he approached, stopping once they were toe-to-toe.

Stumbling, she backed into his father's desk and abruptly sat. He sucked his grin between his teeth. She really hated having her personal space invaded.

"And it's not as if you were going to kiss anyone. At least, not *that* way. Right?"

"Of course! I…mean…of course not!"

"Mmm-hmm." Man, she had incredible eyes. Like blue opals. So light and full of sparks. He glanced at her lips. "Sure."

She pushed some stray strands of hair behind her ears. "Exactly what are you getting at?"

Well, now, that was a good question. He'd taken leave of his senses a while ago, and couldn't be sure what mix of emotion was goading him to goad her.

"Just that you don't really need a breath mint. Unless you were expecting me to give you a brotherly peck on the cheek at the end of the evening. You know how families do."

Their noses were apart by the mere length of a pencil now, and Cynthia had to lean on her palms and strain back over the top of Harrison's desk in order to remain upright. Resting the butts of his hands alongside hers, Rick leaned over, effectively pinning her in place.

The heating unit suddenly clicked off, leaving them in a silence akin to a winter snowfall. For an aeon they stared into each other's eyes, unblinking. Challenging. Each trying to see what was going through the other's mind. Rain *drip, drip, dripped* into the metal gutters and ran into the downspouts just outside the window. The twiggy fingers of a branch scratched at a windowpane in the breeze.

A chill roared down Cynthia's spine.

He brought his lips a hairbreadth from hers and pretended to take a little sniff.

"Mmm. You do smell good enough to kiss, just as you are."

"No, no." Her protest sounded weak to her own ears and she suddenly wished with all her heart that this brutish animal would kiss her. Hard. The kind of kiss she'd never shared with Graham, but yearned for all her life. The kind of kiss that would mess up her hair and devour her lipstick. The kind of kiss that would leave her cheeks abraded and tender from the stubble on his chin. The kind of kiss that would ruin her for any other man.

She felt a wild exhilaration crowding from stomach to throat that she'd never felt before, and she had to fight the impulse to lean forward just enough to taste the sneer on his lips. Instead, she reached up and cupped his steely biceps in the palms of her hands to keep from falling supine across the table, and grappled with her senses.

This was Graham's brother, for heaven's sake. Not to mention the fact that he was looking at her as if she'd been panning for gold in his father's desk. Then why the devil was she so turned on?

The ragged little puffs of her breath rebounded off his lips and his voice came low, feral, against her mouth.

"I don't think Graham would mind if you were planning on kissing me good-night—"

"I wasn't—!"

"After all, we *are* practically related—"

"No—"

"No?"

"No! I mean, yes, we are practically related, but no, I...I...didn't...want...you...to...kiss me...." She closed her eyes against the pull of his glittering eyes and tried to will him into releasing her. Which was hard, as she wanted nothing of the kind.

However, what *he* wanted was something different altogether. Clearly he wanted to punish her for committing what he perceived to be a crime against his family. He wanted to prove with a kiss that she really wasn't after his brother, but after his brother's finances. What better way to demonstrate what he believed to be so obvious?

No. She could not let him kiss her. Under any circumstances.

"Cynthia? Darling? Hmm..." Katherine's feeble voice echoed from the family room into the foyer. "Harrison, sweetheart, perhaps she's lost. Go find her, will you? And while you're up, step into your office for my date book, and something to write with."

The sound of Harrison's loafers approaching and the smell of pipe smoke had them frozen.

"Later, then." Rick's nose grazed hers and he took a step back just as Harrison hummed his way around the corner and into his office. Upon spotting them, he smiled broadly. He seemed not to notice the lightning bolts that crackled between his son and future daughter-in-law.

"Oh, there you kids are. Mother is looking for you both. She's got big plans she wants to discuss." Smile lines forked in the corners of Harrison's eyes and he puffed for a thoughtful moment before he pointed the stem of his pipe at them and spoke again. "You know, I think she's beginning to perk up a bit. This is the first spark I've seen since…well, since long before Dad fell ill. Planning this wedding must be just what the doctor ordered." He chuckled and beckoned for them to follow him back down the hall.

"Not this doctor," Rick muttered.

Unaware that his son had spoken, Harrison called over his shoulder, "Come, join us in the parlor for a smidge longer. Your mother's having a ball with all this brainstorming and that makes me pretty doggone happy."

Cynthia's shoulders drooped as she slogged after Harrison.

Rick watched Cynthia follow his father to the parlor. Before he joined them, though, he decided to give his blood pressure a chance to return to normal. The blood pumping through his body, the beat of his heart, the labored breathing all echoed in his ears. Criminy, what was happening to him? He raked a hand over his jaw and to the back of his neck and silently cursed his weakness.

He'd almost kissed her back there.

For a moment, it was all he'd wanted in this world. To drown in the tropical-sea blue of her eyes and lose himself in the taste of her lips. What the devil was he thinking? She was a *crook,* for pity's sake! Corrupt. Rotten through and through. And though he suspected that Graham and Cynthia's relationship was nothing more than a partnership for profit, he still hated himself for stooping to their level. Even if it meant a kiss could expose this sham of an engagement.

He leaned back against one of the marble pillars that supported the first of two arches leading to the family room. The stone was cool against his back as he crossed his arms and legs and studied the chummy tableau in the family room. Stroking his jaw, he realized that no prescription he could write could have his mother's cheeks such a healthy pink and her eyes sparkling with such unmitigated joy. And Katherine wasn't the only one who enjoyed Cynthia's company. Harrison was fairly beaming at the girl.

And then...there was the matter of himself.

As he stood, wondering at his forbidden attraction to Cynthia, he decided that the problem must be his lack of a personal life. He'd been out of the loop for too long. With a sorry shake of his head, he knew he must be getting pretty hard up if he was falling for one of his brother's shifty sidekicks. Yep. It was time to dust off the little black book and look up some of his old girlfriends. The ones who weren't already married. Or so boring he'd fossilize before the end of a date.

Resurfacing from his reverie, he could hear Cynthia's voice coming from the family room, and again his traitorous body reacted to the sound in ways that were not exactly brotherly.

Miserable, Cynthia looked up from her three-pound copy of *Millennium Wedding* to see Rick enter the room. For the longest time he'd stood hovering beyond the doorway and she knew he'd been watching and listening to every word she spoke.

That had been unnerving enough, but when he finally came into the room and took his place next to her on the love seat, it was even worse. Lazily he lounged against her, crowding her and never removing his dark gaze from her face. Her neck. Her jawline. Her lips.

It was impossible to concentrate on what Katherine was saying, with him staring that way.

He thought she was a thief. He thought he'd caught her

red-handed back there in Harrison's office. Which, of course, he had, but not in the way he thought. He'd walked in on her just as she'd discovered a Post-it note stuck to the ink blotter with Graham's Boston phone number scrawled in Harrison's hand. She'd had time to memorize only five of the seven numbers.

Without calculating the mathematical possibilities, she figured she might be able—with a little luck—to get hold of Graham after only several thousand tries.

She shot Rick a withering glance, which only had him exerting more pressure against her side.

"Do you mind?"

"Not at all." He leaned even more heavily.

In an effort to ignore him, Cynthia focused on Katherine and noticed that the light in her eyes was taking on a fanatical quality. She was really getting into this wedding thing. It seemed that, in the short time that Cynthia had slipped to the bathroom and then to Harrison's office, she'd gone and hired a wedding planner.

Whoa.

Back up.

Now Katherine was talking about a *wedding planner?*

"You…" Cynthia swallowed. Hard. *Stay calm, stay calm, stay calm.* "You hired a, ahem, wedding planner?"

"Yes, Cynthia, darlin'. Just moments ago, while you were out of the room. I called upon the help of a dear friend, whose sister just planned the most marvelous affair and, well, knowing the time crunch we are under, I thought I'd go ahead—"

"A…wedding planner?"

"Of course. Why, I wouldn't dream of doing a wedding without one."

"But, but—"

"No, no, now, hush. It's our treat. You don't need to

thank me, sweetheart! Why, it's my pleasure! Isn't it, Harry?"

"Mmm. Her pleasure."

"But surely we don't need to start planning the wedding now?"

Rick leaned ever closer, his grin mocking. "Why not? You're getting married, aren't you?"

"I...I..."

"Of course she is! She and Graham have been engaged for months! And now that they have such a beautiful place to live, I simply don't see any point in waiting."

Rick slapped Cynthia on the knee. "No point in waiting. Especially considering their...*love.*"

Jaw slack with shock, Cynthia could only stare as Katherine nattered excitedly on about her plans.

The eraser tip of her pencil to her lips, Katherine wondered, "Darlin', when will you be done with fall classes? Although I don't know what difference it makes. It's not like you are going to have to work. Once you and Graham move into the mansion, you'll be a lady of leisure."

A lady of leisure? Cynthia's lips puckered at the thought of emulating the life of Graham's hothouse-flower mother. The last thing on earth she wanted was to be a lady of leisure. If she couldn't find some way to contribute to society, then she might as well toss it in.

"Katherine, I don't want to come off like some kind of—"

"Gold digger?" Rick supplied.

"Ingrate." Baring her teeth at him in a pseudosmile, she planted an elbow in his side. "But I really don't think that we need to get too carried aw—"

"Harrison, darling, when are the Naughtons going to be in town? Didn't Frank say they would be here over the holidays? And what about the Weatherbys? England? It's certainly not too late to schedule people from Europe—"

"Europe?" Cynthia unconsciously clutched Rick's arm.

"And how about David and Lauren Barclay and their children…"

"But Katherine…" A bead of sweat skipped down Cynthia's spine and she shivered. "Honestly, I really, really, *really* think we should wait for Graham—"

"Nonsense. Graham will be delighted that he doesn't have to be bothered with the details."

After a grueling evening spent debating the merits of a seed-pearled-hat-with-netting versus a tiara-with-veil, Cynthia finally managed to convince Katherine that they needed to sleep on this. The fact that Katherine protested, and seemed willing to stay up to the wee hours planning, pleased Harrison immensely.

But Cynthia needed to get home and start trying to find Graham. She also wanted some time alone. To think. To plan how she was going to gently and tactfully get Katherine to hold everything, while at the same time giving Graham a chance to come home and break the news to his parents.

Katherine had really caught her off guard with the wedding planner surprise. Cynthia had been so completely nonplussed that she'd simply gone with the flow. But when it was suggested that a rehearsal dinner at the Space Needle would be grand, and that they simply had to invite the governor, Cynthia knew that she had to bring the evening to an abrupt close.

She retrieved her purse from beneath her feet and stood. She smoothed her skirt and hoped she didn't look as awkward as she felt as she donned a bright smile prepared to bid them goodbye.

"Well, well. Will you look at the time? Gracious! It's past my bedtime. I should probably be on my way. Thank you so much for a lovely evening. Dinner was wonderful. Katherine, I'll be in touch.''

As she backed toward the door and into the hall, she blew air kisses to Graham's parents, ignored the broadly grinning Rick and then, as if the hounds of hell were shredding her Achilles, she fled to the foyer and began to rummage for her coat in the recesses of the hall closet where Rick had thrown it earlier.

Rick and his parents followed and watched her struggle with the wadded wool.

''Rick, darlin', help Cynthia with her wrap, won't you? Somehow it must have slipped off the hanger and become tangled.''

Ever gallant, Rick stepped forward and tried to wrest her coat from her hands.

''Would you back off?'' Cynthia whispered, then turned a thousand-watter on Katherine and Harrison, who hovered over by the stairs.

''Now, now,'' Rick murmured, ''play nice. Mom and Dad are watching and they are under the impression that you are a lovely girl.''

''I *am* a lovely girl.''

''Um-hum.'' To his parents he called, ''You guys go on up to bed. I'll take care of the pleasantries.''

''Good night, Cynthia,'' Harrison and Katherine called as they—arm in arm—mounted the stair.

''And, darlin', drive carefully.'' Katherine stopped at the first landing. ''Harrison, I don't like her driving that old pile of junk of hers. Can't you call and have Jarred drive her home in the limo? Or Rick, why don't you take her home?''

''I'll be fine, Katherine,'' Cynthia insisted. ''Good night! And thank you for dinner!''

Rick reached for the door before she could flee. Blocking her escape, he peeked outside and saw her beat-up car sitting down at the end of the drive, parked at the curb. He frowned. "You really should let me take you home."

"Are you crazy?" she whispered, jeering. "I'm not going anywhere with you."

He lowered his own voice. "Well, then at least give me a good-night hug. My folks are watching."

"No way." She emitted some incredulous laughter at his sheer gall.

"Listen, you saw how thrilled they were that we were getting along so famously. Now, hug me." He ground the words out, forcefully pulling her close.

"Okay, okay." Limply she acquiesced, allowing her arms to flop around his waist.

"Good. Now for that brotherly kiss. Pucker up."

She snorted. "Forget you."

"Now, don't spoil my mother's perfect evening."

Cynthia glanced back at Katherine, who was hovering at the top of the stairs and fairly glowing with happiness.

"Just a little peck. Right here." He pointed to his lips.

"*Sheeyeah.* Like I'm kissing you on the lips. In your dreams, cowboy."

"That's the way we Wingates do it. Now, are you going to stand here all evening and argue with me, or are you going to kiss your loving brother good-night?"

"I don't have a loving brother. I do, however, have a low-down, snake in the gr—"

"Would you shut up?" Rick growled, and cut her diatribe off midstream by crushing his mouth upon hers.

His frustration must have driven him to the brink of insanity, for he hauled her up against his chest and gave her a kiss that left her gasping and his parents smiling quizzically at them—and then frowning quizzically at each other—and then smiling quizzically at them again.

Seeming to realize his mistake just a tad too late, Rick

bellowed, "Welcome to the family, sis," and slapped her on the back.

"You're crazy," she hissed as she slipped into the blustery night.

Yes, Rick had to agree as the door slammed in his face. He was.

Cynthia arrived home to find Tiffany and her baby sitting in the dingy hallway in front of her apartment door. The baby was red faced and crying and there were two paper bags full of clothing sitting on the floor next to them. Tiffany looked frazzled and there was a distinct adult-size handprint on her left cheek. Cynthia dropped her purse on the floor and, crouching low, peered into the young girl's puffy eyes.

"Tiffany! Honey, what in heaven's name are you doing here at this hour?"

Tiffany's smile was watery. She sniffed and wiped her rosy nose on her wrist. "I had a fight with my mom and her boyfriend, and I wondered if I—and Hondo here—could crash with you, since we have nowhere else to go." The teenager jostled her shrieking son.

Named partly for his father's motorcycle and partly for a John Wayne film, little Hondo arched his back, pulled his mother's nose ring and, chubby legs swinging, howled at the ceiling. Tear tracks streaked his dirty cheeks and he looked nearly as exhausted and out of sorts as his mother.

"I…" Cynthia frowned, wondering where on earth she'd put the girl and her little…Hondo. The child was sliding down his mother's body, taking much of her jewelry and clothing with him.

Tiffany sighed. "I understand if it's too much of a hassle…."

"No! No, of course not! I'd love to have the company." The eighteen-month-old Hondo threw himself to the

floor and proceeded to work up a full-fledged tantrum.
Arms thrashing, legs swinging, he vented his hostility to
the greater Seattle area.

One door up the hall, and then another down, creaked
open. Heads poked out and not, it seemed by their scowls,
to wish them to have a nice day.

Cynthia fumbled with her keys, unlocked her door and
hustled them all inside. Rosy Cheeks woke from a sound
sleep and issued a few rusty woofs. Leading with her lower
teeth, the ugly dog eyed the tiny human windmill that was
Hondo with undisguised loathing and growled. Even as she
rebuked her dog, Cynthia knew how the animal felt.

Hondo here was a handful.

Tiffany eyed the bathroom with relief. "Thank heavens!
I gotta go like a racehorse after a victory binge. Here."
She thrust the suspicious, flailing, screaming Hondo into
Cynthia's arms and made a beeline for the toilet.

"Uh, Tiffany, the door doesn't close, uh, there...."

"I don't care," Tiffany called, and proceeded with her
business.

Turning away to give the child some privacy, Cynthia
racked her brain for the sleeping arrangements. Blankets
were in short supply, and it was a little too late in the
evening to knit one for Tiffany and the baby.

And with her bathroom situation... The toilet flushed
and Tiffany moved to the sink and plunged her head, face
first, under the faucet.

Okey-dokey. There was no way they could all sleep at
the same time. As it was, there was barely enough room
for her and Rosy Cheeks. They'd have to take turns.

Exhausted after a day slinging hot fudge, fighting with
Graham's ill-mannered brother and then planning a wedding that would never happen, Cynthia groaned. Sinking
to one of her two dining-table chairs, she tried to disen-

tangle Hondo's fists from her hair, even as she went deaf from his screams.

This was never going to work.

Making a snap decision, she reached over her tiny kitchen table and grabbed the envelope that the lawyer had given her yesterday.

"Tiffany, as soon as you're done in there, grab your stuff and follow me. We're going home."

Chapter Five

"Wow! This is home?" Tiffany kept her awe at a whisper as baby Hondo had finally—and blessedly—nodded off in the car on the way over.

"It is now."

Using her shoulder, Cynthia pushed shut the heavy mahogany doors of Wingate Manor, dropped their bags on the floor and then turned to bring up the preset lighting system inside the foyer. The fabulous home immediately assumed a "for the rich and famous" magazine-cover quality. Rosy Cheeks's nails clicked on the ice-cold marble squares as she trotted around, getting acquainted with the unfamiliar smell of the place.

When they'd first arrived, down at the beginning of the winding drive, Cynthia had informed the security staff of their presence over the intercom in order to forestall an unscheduled visit by the authorities. Wanting privacy, she'd also excused these same people in addition to the night staff and they'd all agreed to retire to their quarters over the monstrous garage, where they lived in a series of luxury apartments.

After she'd pushed in her private code, the iron gates had swung open like enormous welcoming arms. Her single headlight had illuminated the long and winding, tree-lined drive as she and Tiffany had sputtered and putted toward the house. She'd parked her twenty-year-old car under the portico, grabbed the few bags they'd packed and come inside her new home. And here they were.

Home sweet home.

More or less.

They were alone in the cavernous foyer, and even their whispers seemed to have an eerie echo. Cynthia shivered. It was chilly. Especially without Alfred's jolly personality to give the joint some heat. Even with a full staff, it would seem unbearably lonely, now that Alfred was gone. She looked around at the opulence, usually reserved for the most elite hotel lobbies. Someone had thought to decorate for the holidays, and tasteful ornaments hung from a tree—diminutive in this room at a dozen-plus feet—and swags adorned doorways and mantels and the massive stair rail. The sheer elegance was overwhelming.

Cynthia's sigh reverberated with wonder. Would she ever get used to living here by herself?

Doubtful, she decided.

It was neither cluttered nor homey. Nor comfy nor cozy. Not the kind of place where one could shuck one's sweater and shoes by the door and flop on the couch with a cup of coffee and a good book. Her gaze roved over the heavy velvet draperies and the silky tassels, which had to have cost several hundred dollars each. Indirect lighting drew the eye to massive works of art—sculptures, paintings and creations of glass and crystal. The furniture was rare, collectible and imported. Everything was color coordinated in timeless jewel tones and polished to perfection.

Cynthia's gaze followed the double-sided staircase as it curved around her toward the second floor, and she realized that this mausoleum made Katherine and Harrison's swanky digs look positively dowdy. No wonder Katherine had had her heart set on eventually becoming mistress of the mansion that was Wingate Manor. It was easy to picture Graham's mother throwing galas for her various social groups and hosting dignitaries from home and abroad here in this house.

It was for just such reasons that Alfred had it built for his true love.

Again Cynthia tried to puzzle out just why the old man had wanted *her* to have a mansion, of all things. It still made no sense. She was a single college student, with no family save a rather smelly bulldog. And her futon and cable spool table would hardly fit in here. She needed this place the way she needed a hotel in the head.

She turned to glance at Tiffany, and couldn't help but smile at the gaping girl.

"Get out!" Tiffany murmured repeatedly. "Get *out! Get OUT!*"

"I know. That was my reaction when I found out it was mine."

"So what are you still doing in that dinky apartment?"

"You don't think this place is too…big?"

"Shut *up!* You are so rich-much."

Cynthia laughed. "C'mon. I'll turn on the fireplace in your suite and get it warming."

"My suite?" Tiffany giggled as she followed Cynthia up the stairs. "Suh-weet! Hear that, Hondo?" she asked the sleeping child. "We got a suite!"

Once she got the girl and her baby settled in for the night, Cynthia decided to make Alfred's old suite her own, as those were the rooms where she felt the most at home and the least lonely. The bedroom still smelled of Alfred— spicy, manly and a little like love. Like family. Her eyes welled with tears at the sudden onslaught of memories.

He'd been so supportive. And kind. And dear. She missed his sense of humor and his unique way of looking at life. In her twenty-four years, Alfred had been the one person she'd felt had truly been family. It was strange. The moment they met, she'd felt a kindred spirit with the old man, and their bond had grown ever tighter until the moment he died.

As she looked around, Cynthia had the impression that even the room was somehow lonely for the old man. The wheelchair and hospital bed were gone, as were the life support machines and other sundry medical paraphernalia. Everything had been tidied and put to rights and it was as if the past months had never even happened.

She took a deep, ragged breath and dropped her bags on his bed. Pushing the maudlin thoughts away, she found the phone and was determined to talk to Graham, even if it meant climbing into her car and driving from Seattle to Boston that very night.

After a confusing and completely frustrating conversation with an information operator in Massachusetts, she was finally able to determine that there were two hotels with numbers similar to the one she'd seen on Harrison's desk.

She struck gold with the second number. A Graham A. Wingate was registered at the Autumn Leaf Hotel in downtown Boston, but did not answer the phone in his room. Cynthia glanced at the clock and quickly calculated east coast time. Way after midnight. Way, way, *waaaaay* after midnight. For some reason, the fact that Graham was not in his room during the wee hours of the morning didn't really bother her the way it would have before Alfred died.

When the voice mailbox to his room came on, Cynthia went off.

"Graham, it's me. Cynthia. Remember me? Where are you? On second thought, don't answer that. Listen. I've been trying to reach your cell phone, but I can't get through. As soon as you get this message, *call me back!* I need to talk to you!'' Cynthia began to pace, following the raised pattern in the Turkish rug next to Alfred's massive old bed. ''This is never going to work! Do you hear me? We can never pull this off. Sooner or later someone is going to get suspicious about our little…arrangement, and I can't…no, I won't…do this by myself! It's not fair!''

Besides, she fumed, the longer he waited to tell his parents that they were no longer engaged, the bigger the mess they'd have on their hands. Poor, fragile Katherine would never recover from the trauma. Cynthia gripped the phone until her knuckles went white. She adored the ditzy Katherine. And, at Graham's thoughtless insistence, this sham was becoming uncommonly cruel. She wouldn't stand for it.

''You need to come home now and handle this! I can't keep lying to these people forever. Do you understand me? Call me!''

Angrily she slammed the phone into its cradle, then stood fuming for a long, shaky moment. Finally a sound near her door pulled her from her woolgathering. Rosy Cheeks? She looked around. No dog. Silly girl.

''Rosy?'' she whispered.

Silence.

The poor thing was probably hopelessly lost by now.

Gathering her sweater more tightly about her waist, Cynthia headed out of the suite to look for her dog. As she strode into the hallway, something moved in the darkness just outside her room. At first she thought the shadow was Rosy Cheeks, but the absence of clicking toenails had her discount that theory. Rapid-fire, she sorted other possibilities such as Tiffany searching for a glass of water or perhaps a midnight snack, but immediately she realized that this particular shadow was far…far…too…big….

And it was moving.

Toward her.

Crushing her fists to her mouth, she screamed a raspy scream that traveled only as far as her throat. The room swirled and swayed and she just knew that her heart was going to jump out of her chest and beat a path for the hills. Her chest heaved as she panted for precious oxygen. It was as if the floor had turned to Jell-O as she turned and forced herself into motion. *Run!* her brain shrieked, but her legs ignored the command and instead buckled at the knees.

Just before she hit the ground, a pair of steely arms surrounded her waist. Her heart lodged in her throat, prohibiting anything more than a guttural scream. Arms and legs on autopilot now, she fought for all she was worth, kicking and punching and trying to escape this intruder's embrace.

"*Uff!* Cynthia?"

As she pummeled the granite chest with her fists, a vaguely familiar ring to the voice penetrated her terror. She knew this guy from somewhere. She could tell by the voice. And the smell of leather and gasoline and icy weather and mint gum and a hint of...death.

By chocolate.

Rick?

Eyes finally adjusting, Cynthia peered through the gloaming into the handsome face peering back. *Was it really Rick?*

"Cynthia?"

"Rick!" She jerked her arms from his grasp and took a shaky step back. Arm behind her, she fumbled for the wall switch, and suddenly they were bathed in light. "You just scared the pea-waddin' out of me. What on earth are you *doing* here?"

He snorted. "I could ask you the same question."

"No, you can't. This is *my* house."

"So?"

"I ask the questions!"

"You're pretty tough, arncha?"

His amused expression had her hands snapping to her hips.

"Oh, for... Why am I standing here, in the middle of the night, arguing with you? What do you want?"

When he didn't answer right away, she suddenly remembered the phone call she'd just made and wondered just how much of her conversation with Graham's answering machine he'd heard. It would certainly sound incriminating to the uninformed listener.

Stay calm, stay calm, stay calm. She hoped her repetitive mantra would quell the panic she felt rising as she tried to come up with a plausible explanation that would suit both of the brothers Wingate.

Good fortune smiled on her in the form of baby Hondo, and Rick's attention was turned to the squalling boy.

"What was that?" Rick cocked his ear toward the end of the hall and strained to hear the baby's late-night cries.

"What?"

Rick eyed her in the sudden silence and Cynthia knew he was chalking up more evidence against her as a liar. And could she blame him? Not at all. However, the *last* thing she needed right now was for Tiffany to wander out here and blurt out the fact that she and Graham were no longer planning to marry.

Again Hondo shrieked and again Rick's eyes narrowed as he glanced back over his shoulder. "That." Chin to shoulder, he jerked his head in the direction of the sound.

"Oh, *that!*" Cynthia forced a carefree smile. "Sounds like the neighbor's cat, don't you think?"

"The nearest neighbors are a quarter mile away. Must be a big cat."

"Probably."

"Angry cat," Rick said.

"Very."

"Sounds like it needs a diaper change."

Cynthia sighed and shook her head at the ceiling. "Probably." She could tell by his stony expression that he'd figured out there was a baby in the house and was now wondering to whom the baby belonged and if the child's parents were here in the house with her.

She'd reached her tolerance limit with his suspicion.

"Are you going to tell me what you're doing here?" she snapped, but received no answer for her trouble. No sound. No motion. No warmth. Just stony-eyed silence.

Fine. She could outstare him. Though his eyes were normally green, they now appeared almost black, so wide were his pupils. The clock ticked, the sands shifted, the world turned and Cynthia felt naked. Vulnerable. Dissected by his shrewd, unblinking scrutiny. Never had she felt so utterly transparent. It was eerie.

He *knew* her.

In fact, it was almost as if they'd always known each other. As if there was a connection that transcended the time-space continuum. And now he was trying to sort what he knew about her, from what he believed to be true.

Unable to stand the pressure any longer, she lowered her gaze and hoped that he hadn't also been able to see the ridiculous attraction in her eyes. Okay. Enough vulnerability. It was time to take the offensive stance.

"So. You're checking up on me?"

"I didn't know you'd be here."

"Right. Why don't you tell me the truth?"

"Why don't you?"

Ah, yes. The truth. Now, there was a refreshing concept. Cynthia silently cursed Graham's compulsive need to please and protect his mother. "Rick, I'm tired. I've had a long day. Why don't you simply tell me what you want and then we can go to bed.''

Rick raised a roguish brow and, realizing what she'd said, she felt the heat sting her face and backpedaled. "*You* can go to bed. At *your* house. In *your* bed.''

A small grin curled his lips. When he finally spoke, it was with quiet tenderness. ''I came over because I was remembering.''

''Remembering what?''

''Him.''

A profound sadness creased his brow and the corners of his mouth. His obvious pain was a surprise to Cynthia. She didn't think he had it in him to care so deeply. Graham had displayed no such emotion when Alfred had passed. Yet another difference between the two Wingate brothers, she noted.

''Isn't it kind of late for a trip down memory lane?''

''I couldn't sleep. And I really didn't think you'd be here.''

''How did you get past security?''

''They know me.''

''Ah.''

''I didn't make it home in time for the memorial, and I just wanted…to see, to feel…'' He sighed. ''I don't know what I wanted.'' Something in his voice had changed. Softened. For once, he was not sarcastic.

''Yes, I—I know what you mean.'' A shard of ice in her heart began to thaw where he was concerned, and he looked at her as if he believed she truly did empathize—in Alfred's case, anyway.

Face-to-face, they hovered in the hall, regarding each other with tentative understanding. New and not completely unpleasant feelings were beginning to take root, as they'd shared a mutual loss and now an understanding of each other's sorrow.

"Would you like to go into Alfred's room? You know, to pay your respects, or whatever?"

"I— Isn't that your new room?"

"Yes."

"Ahhh, no."

"Why not?"

"That might not seem proper."

"Proper?" As if breaking and entering was proper. He always found a way to make her look a moral moron. She shrugged. "Suit yourself."

"I always do."

"Listen." She sighed. "There is a lot of Alfred's personal stuff to sort, up in the attic. Later, if you want to see if there are any meaningful mementos from his life that you'd like to have, that would be fine with me. Otherwise, just...stay away."

"When?"

"I'm crazy busy till Wednesday, when I only have two morning classes. So sometime that afternoon would be fine. Call before you come over, to make sure I'm here. Please."

Without actually acquiescing, he nodded, and Cynthia wondered if he'd show up.

He took a step backward, and she felt herself leaning toward him, even as he turned and headed to the top of the stairs.

"Good night," was all he mumbled, but it was enough to keep Cynthia riveted to her spot for the longest time, replaying the sound and inflection of his voice. Taking the steps two at a time, Rick disappeared into the night, slamming the heavy doors after him and then shooting the bolt lock with his key.

"Good night," she called, knowing he couldn't hear but wanting that connection. As his headlights swung around, lighting the hall walls, then her face and then the trees

outdoors, she thought about Rick Wingate and almost...
almost wished that she'd met him first.

As he wove his way down Wingate Manor's endless
drive, Rick knew he had a problem. He'd overheard
enough of Cynthia's phone call to Graham to know that
the two of them were up to something. Unfortunately, he
hadn't heard enough hard evidence to actually incriminate
them in anything specific. He guessed it didn't really matter. At least, not as far as he was concerned.

She was trouble.

For reasons of sanity and family harmony—and all that
was holy—he needed to steer clear of her.

However, in the most secret recesses of his heart he
yearned to possess Cynthia in a way that rivaled the bib-
lical David's desire for Bathsheba. And though Cynthia
was certainly no more available than Bathsheba had been,
this in no way quelled his desperate desire.

As he turned out of the driveway and onto the hilltop
lane that led to downtown Seattle, he gave his head a sharp
shake. What the devil was happening to him? So far, he
was the third chump in this family she'd managed to snare
under her sexy spell.

And his parents were no better.

His mother fairly glowed with happiness over this whole
wedding debacle and his father was glowing over his
mother's glow. He tightened his fingers around the steering
wheel. There would be all manner of emotional hell to pay
when she finally ditched them all and headed for new pastures the color of money.

He could only be grateful that Cynthia was Graham's
problem.

At least as far as anyone else knew.

The following Wednesday found Cynthia—after two
morning classes—crouched on the dusty floor of Alfred's

attic, rummaging through boxes of photos and World War II mementos. Three days had passed since she'd left the message with Graham, yet still no word. As a distraction from her predicament, she'd thrown herself into the cleaning and sorting mode.

A red bandanna, meant to keep the dust from her hair, sported several longish cobwebs. Streaks of dirt and grime on her nose and cheeks went unnoticed as she pored over the history spread out before her.

Alfred had led such a colorful life. Travel, wine, women, song... She squinted at a photo of a young, handsome Alfred in uniform, posing with a bevy of beauties in old-fashioned swimsuits and flowered bathing caps. The flirtatious quirk at his brow was Graham's.

The rugged build was Rick's.

She peered a little closer. Ahhh. So *that's* where Rick got that broad chest and those corded arms and thighs. She was beginning to understand what old Mrs. Meier had meant about Alfred cutting quite the dashing figure of a man in his youth. He *was* pretty cute. But not as sexy and dangerous as his firstborn grandson.

A groan rumbled at the ridiculous direction her thoughts had taken and, feeling suddenly sore and cramped from sitting in one position for so long, Cynthia leaned back to stretch and yawn. A glance around at the mountain of boxes containing photos and slides and clothing and other memorabilia had her wondering at the sanity of giving the staff this time before the holidays off. But she'd wanted to be by herself. To grieve. To explore. To remember.

She checked her watch and then Hondo, who was sitting nearby busily shredding an old pile of magazines. Rosy Cheeks lay under an old dresser, watching with suspicion in her watery eyes. This morning, when Hondo's mother had left him with Cynthia—so she could pull a morning shift at Pudgie's—the boy had pitched only one tantrum.

But it had been a doozy.

The tears and heart-wrenching sobs had lasted two hours easily, after he'd woken and discovered his mother gone. Cynthia had rocked, paced, sung, pranced, joggled, jiggled, made silly noises, but all to no avail. Hondo, it seemed, had needed a good, lung-clearing cry.

She knew the feeling.

Since then, he'd been reasonably content—a few crying jags notwithstanding—with some old odds and ends to destroy.

Counting on her fingers, Cynthia figured that Tiffany should be home within two—three at the most—hours. And Rick? Should have been here by now.

A surge of silly disappointment settled in her belly. She didn't know why she'd expected him to show up. It wasn't as if they'd made some kind of date. Still, she'd looked forward to his company. Rude and accusatory as it was, it was better than nothing.

With a heavy sigh, Cynthia reached for a box and slid it across the floor to her side. Listlessly she poked about inside and came out with a stack of letters tied up with faded yellow ribbon. She frowned. What was this?

Setting the pile on her lap, she leaned back against a support beam and crossed her ankles. After wrestling with the ancient knot, she withdrew a letter from the top of the stack and examined the postmark. Wow. Nearly sixty years had passed since this letter had been sent. The paper was brittle with age, and gingerly she slid her finger beneath the flap and coaxed it open.

Someone named Jayne had written this letter. Cynthia's brows formed one fine line as she unfolded the ancient stationery.

Jayne?

Odd. Rick's grandmother was Elaine. A flash of excitement traveled up Cynthia's spine. Could this be from Alfred's first love? The woman for whom he went to his grave filled with regret over letting her go?

The spidery hand flowed across the page in a most artistic manner and the going was slow as Cynthia struggled to decipher each tender passage.

"My Daring Alfred…"

Cynthia gnawed on her bottom lip. Daring? She held the letter up to the light. Ah. Darling. That made more sense.

"My *Darling* Alfred…"

Her eyes followed the swoops and swirls and she mouthed each word out loud.

"'I like feathers since you sent soft…pillows?'"

Cynthia frowned. No, that couldn't be right. Hmm. She'd just have to continue scanning the missive till she got the hang of this Jayne woman's indistinct scrawl.

Mother says I'm not eating or washing…something terrible happened and…something, something… Muffy and Fluffy want to marry Thomas. When I die just go out to the pastures of hoppy snacks….

Good grief. With a clearing blink of her eyes, Cynthia began again, slowly taking one fancified letter at a time.

My Darling Alfred:
It seems like forever since you set sail for the South Pacific. Mother says I've been moping about like a spoiled child, not eating, not sleeping, but instead wishing you were here. I miss you something terribly, and am hoping that you will return soon. Mother and Father still want me to marry Thomas, but I refuse! I'd sooner die. I must go now, and put on the pretense

of happiness. Please write to me as soon as you can,
as I live for your letters. Until you return to me,
Lovingly,
Your Jayne forever

Cynthia swiped at a tear. How sad. She wondered if
there was a picture of her here, among his things. This
Jayne had to be his first and only true love. The one he
built the house for. The sacred one, whose name he could
no longer bring himself to utter.

A light tap on her shoulder had her screaming with
fright. Letters flew every which way and the box on her
lap upended, scattering its contents all over the floor.
Lower lip quivering, baby Hondo's face puckered and
Rosy Cheeks issued a few belated barks.

"Rick!" Bosom heaving, Cynthia clutched the placket
where her blouse met her throat and tried to bring her pulse
under control. With an accusatory finger, she pointed.
"You said you were going to call before you came."

"I did."

On shaky legs she stood and crossed to retrieve the now-
squalling Hondo. She hiked the frightened child up to her
hip and expertly avoided his fists and feet as he attempted
to ascend her torso and wrap himself around her neck.
With his tiny fists the baby tore her scarf out of her hair
and her hair out of her bun. She managed to hold him off
before he pulled the bun out of her head. Completely bedraggled, she heaved a resigned sigh. "You did? When?"

"'Bout an hour ago. It rang several times and finally
the machine picked up. I left you a message." He reached
down to the top of a packing crate for her wireless phone
and flipped a switch. "These things work better when
they're on."

"Oh. Right." She ducked her head so that he couldn't

see her idiotic pleasure at his arrival. Big mistake. Hondo's escape plan caught her in the nose. *"Owww!"*

"Hey, you." Rick stepped forward and took the child from her arms. "That's a no-no. We don't hit. No hit."

Warily Hondo stared up at Rick, clearly considering the logistics of smacking this frowning adult.

"Don't even think of it," Rick warned. "No hit. Not nice."

Hondo scowled and beat on Rick's chest with his fists. "No hit!"

"That's right." Rick grinned. "So. I'm Rick. Who are you?"

Still pinching her smarting nose, Cynthia made introductions. "Rick Wingate, this is Hondo Hunter, Tiffany's son."

"Ahhh. Your mommy is the one with the nose ring and the pink hair."

"Yeah. She's a real conservative. Like you."

"Don't let what you see on the outside fool you, Hondo. It's what's inside that counts."

"True." She narrowed her eyes at him, hoping he understood the meaning of his words where she was concerned.

"That's why I said it." He squinted back.

"Good."

"Good."

"Good!"

They stared each other down for a while, as was becoming their custom. Then a simultaneous smile radiated between them, infecting even the fussy Hondo, who bestowed on them a sparsely toothed grin.

"So. What are you doing?" Rick gestured to the mess.

"Sorting. I found some really cool letters to Alfred from some woman named Jayne."

"Really?"

"Um-hum. I think she is the one he built this house for."

"How do you know that?"

"He told me all about her. On the day we met. We used to have long talks about his childhood and his career and some unnamed, unrequited love—now I'm guessing her name was Jayne—and his war experiences, among other things. Sometimes he would dictate stuff to me and I'd jot it down in one of his journals. He was a fascinating guy."

"I guess so."

A tiny pang of jealousy echoed in his words and Cynthia wondered if Rick didn't envy her time together with his grandfather.

Hondo strained to get down, so Rick set him on the floor along with an old baseball he'd found in an open trunk, left over from his own childhood. Happy with his new toy, the child set about terrorizing Rosy Cheeks.

"Baaa!" Hondo screamed, and flung the ball at the dog.

Rosy Cheeks whimpered and slunk farther beneath the antique dresser.

"I'm surprised Alfred kept that old ball. That was from a championship game, back in high school."

"He was very proud of you."

"No. Not really." Rick scratched the stubble at his jaw. Though his lips denied, his eyes held curiosity.

"Yes. He was. Of you, especially. He used to talk about you all the time. I'd read your letters out loud to him quite often, and it always took forever, as he would constantly interrupt to brag about you, or to go on about his own time spent overseas. It was fascinating. And part of the reason, really, that I decided to major in foreign languages."

"No kidding."

"Um-hum. Both of you led such exotic lives...." She sighed. "I guess I figured if I couldn't go there, at least I could learn to talk to the people."

"Maybe someday you'll go."

"I doubt it. I'm not that well fixed."

Rick hooted at that. "You have this house."

She shrugged. "For now."

"Graham travels on business. You could go with him."

"Whatever." Cynthia bent to collect the scattered letters. She didn't want to talk about Graham.

Without ceremony she took her seat on the floor and began to organize the letters by date. When he tossed down his coat and sat not too far from her, she bit back a smile. He would be here for a while. Good. She would enjoy company that did more than babble and bark.

"So. Where do you recommend I begin?"

He looked so bewildered she handed him the letter she'd been reading. "Here. This is the letter from Jayne I was telling you about."

"Mmm." He leaned back against an old trunk. Crossing his legs at the ankles, he unfolded the yellowed paper and began to read aloud. "'My daring Alfred.' Daring?" he murmured, his expression quizzical.

"Darling."

"Yes?" He arched a roguish brow.

"Not you." Cynthia rolled her eyes. "The letter. My *darling* Alfred. The handwriting takes a little getting used to."

"I'll say. Says here she likes the flowers he sent from the soybean parakeet."

Cynthia fell back on her elbows and laughed at the ceiling. A curious Hondo crawled over and parked his tiny body in her lap. "That's not what it says."

"Okay, fine. You're the language expert—you read it to me."

And so she did. And then another and another. It was slow yet fascinating going.

"I had no idea he was so in love with this Jayne person,'' Rick murmured, now reclining in a most relaxed fashion on an old pile of wool army blankets.

"Oh, yes. They were soul mates."

"Why didn't they just get married?"

"According to Alfred, her family had betrothed her to another man. Some guy named Thomas, for financial and political alliances between the families. I think he proposed, but something went wrong. Anyway, she tried to tell Alfred that she didn't care about her family's demands and that she'd run away with him, but Alfred was a proud man. He felt that her family didn't think he was worthy, and that rankled. So he set off to prove them wrong, by making his own fortune. Then the war broke out and he was unable to come home for a long time. By the time he returned, Jayne was married to Thomas, and expecting their first child."

"Bummer."

"Yeah. Just goes to show you that you have to follow your heart."

"Is that what you are doing?"

Cynthia knew he was referring to her relationship with Graham, and so she answered honestly. "Yes." Someday he would understand.

Rick looked at her for a long hard moment before his eyes dropped to the baby in her lap. "He's asleep."

"He's had a hard day crying."

"What's wrong? He sick?" Rick pushed himself off the blanket pile and, crouching next to her, gently probed the child's head for fever.

"I don't think so. I think he's just feeling a little displaced." She pressed her lips to his forehead. "Poor kid. I know exactly how he feels. I grew up in a number of foster homes. It's tough when you don't know where you are or who you're with half the time."

Slowly Rick nodded. "I've seen that look on some of my patients' faces."

Cynthia slid her arms under Hondo's pudgy body and drew the small boy to her chest. He was as floppy as a rag doll, arms and legs limp and hanging, jaw slack, eyes closed. His face was cherubic in repose. Soft, cinnamon-apple cheeks, full rosebud lips, long dark lashes and black curly hair, thick as sheep's wool. The sheer beauty brought a lump to Cynthia's throat and her eyes shone with tears as she smiled up at Rick, who was hovering at her shoulder. Her smile was wobbly. She sniffed.

"No one should ever feel so alone," she murmured brokenly, referring to both Hondo and Alfred and perhaps herself.

"No." Their eyes held for another eternity, but this time there were softer feelings behind the look. The tentative relational roots that had taken hold last time they were together had multiplied between them and a green shoot or two were poking through the soil, seeking warmth. Nourishment. Sustenance.

Valiantly they fought against these flowering feelings. Feelings that Cynthia knew would only further complicate an already far too complicated mess. She tried to tell herself that even though she'd broken it off with Graham, Rick was still something of a brother to her and, in that respect, taboo. Allowing these embers to flare would only lead to heartache. In his eyes she could see him waging the same battle. And losing.

Slowly, gently, Rick ran his hand down her back, lightly rubbing, telling her with his fingertips that he understood. Both the baby and her.

What started out as an awkward pat on the back suddenly became so much more. Hating herself for her neediness, Cynthia leaned against his side, seeking his warmth, his strength. The human connection that she'd longed for

since she'd been a very little girl. Automatically his arm
went to her shoulders and he pulled her close.

There Cynthia finally allowed herself to grieve. For Alfred. For her lost childhood. For lost loves. For Tiffany's
poor choices. For her own. And there, burrowed beneath
Rick's strong arm, she began the long healing process.

While she sobbed, Hondo slept the sleep of the truly
weary.

She did not resist as Rick scooted around behind her,
pulling her between his legs and back against his chest.
With low, soothing words he wrapped her and the baby in
his arms and rocked them. Stroked her hair. Nuzzled her
neck. When his lips found her temple, Cynthia's eyes slid
shut and a shiver ran the length of her spine.

Allowing herself the luxury of his touch, she nestled
ever closer, loving the contact, reveling in the feel of his
biceps beneath her cheek and his chest supporting her
back.

His warm mouth traveled from her temple to her jaw,
planting little soothing butterfly kisses that at once com-
forted and excited. Leaning back, she angled her head to
look up at him, and found in his eyes a reflection of her
own desire.

Her breathing quickened. As did his. Her heart pounded.
As did his. She clutched his arms in the palms of her hands
and offered her mouth to him. He debated only a second
before he took her up on her offer and lowered his lips to
hers.

The kiss, so gentle, so sexy, so volcanic in the way it
turned her entire body to hot liquid, was over far sooner
than she wanted, as the phone, now sitting on a crate next
to their heads, issued a shrill demand for attention.

Cynthia groaned.

Rick groaned.

Hondo groaned.

Reluctantly Rick reached for the phone and handed it to Cynthia, who pressed the on button.

"Hello?" She froze at the sound of the voice on the other end. "Graham?"

Chapter Six

Graham was on the line.

Rick stiffened.

His brother. His own flesh and blood. And though Graham might be a scoundrel and a womanizer, Rick could honestly say at this moment, with his nose buried in the silky sweetness of Cynthia's hair, he was no better. Slowly he loosened his hold at her slender waist and, scooting back, gripped one of the attic's support beams and hauled himself to his feet.

He thrust his hands through his hair and allowed his head to fall back on his shoulders. What a mess. Guilt, hot and heavy, swelled in his gut and into his throat.

He'd been kissing his brother's fiancée.

The woman who would soon become his sister-in-law, for pity's sake. The sister-in-law who was in cahoots to bilk his family out of a fortune in inheritance alone. He exhaled at the ceiling and listened to Cynthia's side of the conversation.

"Where on earth have you been? I've been trying to reach you for days!"

Head cradled in her palms, she leaned over the sleeping baby and rubbed her eyes as she listened to Graham's myriad excuses.

"Right… Okay… Sure. Whatever. Listen, I meant what I said the other night. You need to come home. Now… What do you mean, two more weeks? That's almost Christmas! This is an emergency!… *Why?* What do you mean, *'Why?'* Because your mother is beginning to plan our wedding, that's why. For the day before Christmas Eve…. What do you mean, *'So?'* Did you hear me? She is *planning our wedding!*… Because, considering our previous discussion, it's not fair, that's why…. No! No. I've told you that already. A million times *no!*"

Cynthia glanced up at Rick, and then back down to the dusty plank floor. She drew a listless pattern in the gray silt with her finger.

"Listen, I have to go. I have…company…. Yes. I'm at Alfred's place…. Yes. Where are you going to be staying?… You're still going to Paris? For the love of…when will you know that number?… Okay. Fine…. No. Fine. Call me. Call your *mother*…. Yes, I understand this makes her happy…. Yes, I understand her health is improving…. Yes, that makes me happy, too. But for how long? She has to face the facts…. Now, Graham. It has to come from you. Now."

Rick knew that he should have left when she began this convoluted conversation, but for some reason, his boots were riveted to the floor. He wanted desperately to hear something that he could cling to as a shred of hope for Cynthia's character. But the content was so nebulous that again he was at a complete loss.

That she did not want Katherine planning the wedding was, however, quite clear.

There were also serious problems in her relationship

with Graham. Secrets that spelled trouble. But what?
And why?

Didn't matter. His own morals dictated that he not be
part of those problems. He'd been playing with fire this
afternoon, and he wouldn't be a bit surprised if he'd already been burned. He bent down to gather his leather
jacket from the floor.

"Graham, I'm getting another call. I have to go. Call
your mother!"

No parting endearments, Rick noted. He hated the satisfaction that gave him.

With a sigh that spoke of an incredible weariness, Cynthia pushed the call-waiting button. "Hello? Oh, hello,
Katherine."

Arms up, jacket in midair, Rick again froze. His mother?

"No, no, you're not interrupting…anything."

Lips trembling, Cynthia fixed Rick with a brief, despondent look. Again crushing guilt burned in his throat
as his jacket slid down his arms.

"The…uh, wedding planner? I—I—I—uh, well…I…"
Cynthia fell silent as the excited voice of his mother burbled across the line and into the room. Katherine sounded
full of joy. Life. Truly excited and happy for the first time
in…years.

Cynthia tried to interject.

"But… Yes, but I… Oh? But…But… But… Oh?"

However, Katherine was on a roll.

Slowly Rick shrugged into his jacket, his need to go
only slightly overshadowed by his compulsion to stay. He
made a show of zipping up and finding his motorcycle
helmet.

Shoulders flagging, head bowed beneath the weight of
whatever her predicament was, Cynthia began to nod.
"Sure. I understand…. No, really…it's just that I… Um-

hum, sure…. Once in a lifetime? That is special…. I see…. Right…. Uh-huh…. Yes, I can be there Friday afternoon. Around 4:30?… Okay. See you then.''

Cynthia pushed the off button on the phone and sat staring at the wall. Hondo stirred slightly in her lap and as she absently stroked his downy curls, she spoke to Rick.

''That—'' she waved the phone around and tried to smile ''—was your brother. And, uh, your mother.''

''So I gathered.''

Rick knew he should go before she could lie to him about what had just gone on over the phone, but still, he couldn't seem to muster the wherewithal.

The winter twilight sun slanted through the attic window, bathing Cynthia and the baby in a gold, enchanting light. Lazy dust motes floated in these rays, oblivious to the tension in the room. Her hair fell from a loose bun, giving her a sexy, messy, very girlish appearance. A look that screamed innocence. Could it be? Floorboards squeaked as Rick shifted from one foot to the other, wondering.

Unable to sustain eye contact with her after what had transpired before the phone rang, he allowed his gaze to scan the backside of the lath walls where the plaster oozed and insulation clung. It was a typical attic, filled with trunks and dress dummies and Christmas decorations too ugly or broken for this season. A macaroni wreath, spray painted gold and glued to a cardboard ring, which Rick had made in the fourth grade, lay atop a box of Santas fashioned of clothespins and yarn. Ghosts of another era haunted this place—lost loves, broken dreams and now, betrayal of his brother's trust.

Her voice was low and deadpan as she broke the silence. ''I think it would probably be best if in the future we stayed away from each other.''

''Right.'' Rick balanced his helmet on a hip with his

arm. "Although that's going to be kind of difficult, being that you are marrying into my family."

"Just go."

"If you keep ordering me out of your house this way, I'm going to get a complex."

"Go!"

Hondo whimpered in his sleep.

Without another word, he turned and headed down the stairs. Once Rick was on the road, the frigid air slapped his cheeks and whipped his hair as he flew. With this head-clearing wind in his face, he knew that—now more than ever—he needed to stay near Cynthia. Though it would probably be the end of his now-tenuous hold on sanity, he had to see for himself if she was truly, in her heart of hearts, pledged to his brother.

And if not, was she beyond redemption?

This was it, Cynthia decided as she hovered in the archway that led to Katherine's kitchen. It was time to tell Katherine the truth.

Regardless of Graham's wrath.

Or Katherine's happiness.

Right was right. And wrong was wrong. And Katherine's happiness was just plain wrong.

Wasn't it?

Head virtually exploding with pain and confusion, Cynthia tried to swallow around the wool mitten that had become her tongue. This was simply horrible. Of all the women in the world to hurt, why did it have to be the only one who'd ever treated her like a daughter?

It had been two days, and obviously Graham had neglected to call his mother. Her eyes scanned the giddy scene before her and she battled her frustration with his constant selfishness. On the large granite-topped island sat a plethora of open books, magazines and picture portfolios from Seattle's finest florists, caterers and photographers. Katherine and a woman Cynthia had never seen before were gushing and palavering over these books with a fervor usually reserved for the induction of the new Miss America.

Finally sensing Cynthia's presence, Katherine spun around and spied her future daughter-in-law.

"Ah! Cynthia! Darlin', you're here!" Beaming like Scotty's transporter, Katherine rushed to Cynthia's side and pulled her into the room. "Marcella Edgewater, I'd like you to meet the bride, Cynthia Noble, my future daughter-in-law. Cynthia, this is your wedding planner. Seattle's best."

Bracelets jangling, Marcella flew across the room and, taking Cynthia's hands in hers, pressed them to her ample bosom. "Cynthia, how wonderful to meet you," she chirped, bringing her face so close, her beakish nose went out of focus. Her breath smelled of coffee and cigarettes and there was a bit of something lodged in the good-size gap between her huge front teeth. "Have I got plans for you, girlfriend."

Her arm tucked firmly around Cynthia's waist, she hustled her to the counter and wedged Cynthia between herself and Katherine. "Just before you got here, Katherine and I were testing some catering samples I brought with me. Try this." Lunging forward—and taking Cynthia with her—she dived at a plate of cheese and crackers. Marcella pressed a lump of Brie into Cynthia's mouth before she could protest that she abhorred Brie.

"Huh? Huh? How about that, huh?"

Busily forcing the slithery stuff down her throat, Cynthia could only nod.

Katherine wriggled with excitement and leaned across Cynthia to drag a bowl across the counter. "Marcella, give her some of the caviar!"

Cynthia's gag reflex began to work. She'd never been overly fond of seafood, and their eggs spawned even less enthusiasm.

"Here, doll, try this." Again Marcella force-fed her. "Huh? Huh? How about that?" Beak leading, she peered into Cynthia's face. *"Huhhh?"*

The smell of Brie and fish eggs on Marcella's rancid breath had Cynthia's eyes watering. "Oh, um, yeah, um-hum." Cynthia tried to back away, but Marcella wouldn't hear of it.

The charms on her heavy bracelets jangled as she went into her spiel. The wedding planner seemed to have Katherine in a trance. Her throaty voice, her mesmerizing eyes, her lack of understanding that a person needed at least three feet of personal space—wasn't this the American standard?—was driving Cynthia half out of her mind.

Call it claustrophobia, call it shyness, call it halitosis, but Cynthia needed her space. Now.

"And for the reception I was thinking of giving the guests a choice of lobster, duck *à l'orange,* or prime rib."

"Yes, but what about the vegans?" Katherine was making furious notes in her PalmPilot.

"A bit of penne pasta and grilled Portobello mushrooms?"

"Perfect!"

Cynthia's mouth dropped. One meal alone would cost more than her monthly rent at the apartment. She couldn't let this continue. She had to speak with Katherine. Somehow she had to put a halt to these ridiculous plans.

But how? When? Rearing back, she tried to get a good look at Katherine's face. Her blissful countenance was remarkable. Graham was absolutely right on this count, at least. It seemed that Katherine had finally come out of her chronic depression and was focusing on life again. The

idea of crushing all of her fun was growing more loath-
some by the moment.

Besides, Cynthia fumed, that was Graham's job.

Suddenly the hairs on the back of her neck began to
tingle and her stomach felt as if it were riding a roller
coaster. Upside down.

Rick.

She turned and saw that her sixth sense was accurate—
as usual—where he was concerned.

"Hello, ladies. Mom." He moved behind his mother to
kiss first her cheek and then Cynthia's. "Cyn." A burning
tingle flashed down her spine as his low voice filled her
ear. Memories of the kiss they had shared assailed her and
she couldn't meet his eyes.

Clearly he had no intention of obeying her request that
they stay away from each other.

Marcella dropped Katherine's and Cynthia's hands and
turned to crush Rick in one of her aromatic bear hugs.

"You must be the groom," Marcella gushed.

Cynthia noted his wrinkled nose and had to turn away
to keep from issuing some politically incorrect laughter
born of hysteria.

Rick shook his head. "Actually—"

"Aren't you going to be ab-so-loot-ly *faboo* in a tux?"

He had to hunch over as Marcella yanked his arm and
tucked it under hers, then grabbed Cynthia and dragged
them both over to her overstuffed date planner.

"Speaking of which, I've made an appointment for a
fitting for each of you first thing tomorrow morning at
9:00 a.m. sharp with The Phillip Michael Allen Wedding
Boutique. A miracle, I tell you, as the man is booked until
well into the next decade!" She drew all of their faces
together and said huskily, "Isn't that exciting?"

From over their shoulders Katherine's gentle laughter

burbled. "Marcella, this is my other son, Rick. He is not the groom. Yet."

"Oh?" Marcella's smile grew predatory, and for reasons that she couldn't fathom, Cynthia experienced a pang of jealousy.

Katherine nodded and gave her son's cheek a fond pat. "We've nagged, but he's something of a rogue. However, I know, as a favor to me, he'll be glad to stand in for his brother for the fitting tomorrow, as he and Graham are roughly the same size."

Cynthia stared at Katherine. Was the woman blind? Rick and Graham hadn't been the same size since they were in nappies. If Rick stood in for the fitting, the tux would hang on Graham....

Then again, it wasn't as if Graham was actually going to wear the dumb thing.

She angled her head to find Rick watching her, and tried to decipher what was going on behind those green eyes. Earlier that week he'd overheard the argument between her and Graham and then the conversation with Katherine. A single cell amoeba could see that there was trouble in paradise and that she did not want Katherine planning this calamity.

"Graham call lately, Mom?" With exaggerated casualness, Rick snagged a cracker and loaded it with Brie.

"Good, huh? Huh? Huh?" Marcella panted, arching toward him. "Huhhhh? Try the caviar, too, hon."

"No, dear. I haven't heard from him for...days. He's very busy right now. I don't expect to hear from him for at least a week."

"Ah." He glanced over the top of Marcella's teased and sprayed do, and lifted a brow in Cynthia's direction.

She seethed. He was wondering if she was going to continue to allow his mother to plan her wedding even though she'd encouraged Graham to call a halt to the proceedings.

For some stupid reason, her feelings were hurt. She'd thought they'd come to some kind of meeting of the minds—or at least the lips—but it seemed that he was still suspicious of her true intentions. Couldn't he tell by now that she'd never intentionally hurt Katherine?

Although she could hardly find fault with his thought processes. It wasn't as if he could read her mind. He didn't know that she'd broken up with Graham, and she couldn't tell him. Not yet. Still, she nursed unreasonable feelings of wounded pride. Surely he could see she wasn't some kind of philanderer.

Then again, perhaps that was just what he'd set out to prove.

Her face burned with shame. And with that short but mercury-melting kiss he'd done just that. Well, in that case, let him think what he wanted. He was never going to trust her, so why even try? For now, she would carry on according to Graham's wishes and only hope and pray that he'd soon call his mother and put an end to this debacle. Worst case scenario, she guessed she could pay for the wedding clothes out of her Pudgie's tips and use the silly things when—and if—she ever got married. She hoped Phillip Michael Allen had some sort of long-term payment plan.

"Ooo. I'm sure your standing in for your brother would be just f-i-i-ine." Marcella tapped her lower lip with her pen and inspected his physique under the guise of professional interest.

Again Cynthia had the urge to deck the wedding planner.

Rick shrugged. "I have nothing better to do. Glad to pitch in where I can. It isn't every day a guy's brother gets married. In fact, I have some errands to run tomorrow, so

I'll be happy to swing by and pick up Cynthia on my way to the fitting.''

Cynthia shot him a withering glance. He was going to dog her with his seduction routine until she spilled the beans about her engagement to Graham. Well, it was no use. She could resist him. Now that she knew what he was up to.

"Wonderful!" Katherine clapped her hands with glee and looked back and forth between Cynthia and her eldest son. "Graham will be so happy that you two have taken to each other this way."

Cynthia felt her cheeks blaze like the coils in a potter's kiln.

"Oh, that we have," Rick agreed. "Just like kissin' cousins, huh, Cyn?"

"Ooo, I wish I was your cousin, hon." Revealing a slash of lipstick on her teeth, Marcella grinned. She slammed her date planner shut and glanced at her watch. "I have to run. I'll see you kids again tomorrow after the fitting to talk flowers. Here? Say sevenish?"

"Tomorrow?" The granite countertop was cool beneath Cynthia's deathly grip. "What's the rush?"

"Doll face, are you kidding? With the holidays looming, you'll be lucky to get weeds."

"Can't have that. We'll be here." Rick gave Marcella the thumbs-up.

The following morning found Rick in his parents' driveway polishing his silver-gray Mercedes—his only concession to crass materialism—and thinking of Cynthia. She was right. He needed to stay away from her, but, and this was the rub, how could he keep an eye on her if he did?

Figuring out what was going on between her and Graham had become a bit of an obsession. Then again, as he doused a rag with wax, he had to wonder if he was really interested in keeping an eye on her as a possible perpetrator, or if he was interested in her as a romantic relationship.

She was one sexy woman.

Even though the air was cool, rivulets of sweat began to run down his back and chest as he redoubled his vigorous polishing efforts. Grunts, born of frustration, erupted from his throat as he worked. His shirt clung to his body, and he raised an arm to wipe his brow. Yep, there was something about Cynthia.

When he'd kissed her, she'd kissed back. With feeling. There'd been no mistaking that. No faking. There was something very arousing burning between them, and—as much as he wanted to—Rick just couldn't chalk it all up to her being a user. Something told him that though the circumstances screamed otherwise, Cynthia was not the flake she appeared.

Rick studied his reflection in the gleaming hood of his car. So. What *was* going on?

This much he knew—on one hand, she didn't love Graham. On the other hand, she seemed to have genuine feelings for *him*. On the *other* hand, she was allowing his mother to plan a wedding to his brother.

His heavy sigh fogged his reflection.

Why?

Whatever their kooky relationship, she was—for now, anyway—Graham's woman, and he had to remember that. Plus, even if Graham were out of the picture, Rick knew he needed the kind of woman who would be interested in his unusual type of work. Getting hooked on a hometown girl, one chained to a mansion, and especially one with baggage connected to his family, would never suit his purposes.

He needed a woman free of all that stuff. He needed a woman who could understand his commitment to his work. One who was not afraid to do without the finer things in life. One who wouldn't mind living in squalor in a foreign country.

Rick needed someone with courage. With pluck. Backbone. He needed someone with a sense of humor. Someone who would pick herself up after having been knocked down by life's injustices.

In short, he needed—he squeezed his eyes tightly shut—Cynthia.

When they weren't fighting, they were very comfortable with each other, yet at the same time electrified. It was eerie. Weird. Almost as if they shared a secret past. As if they were soul mates of some kind.

Just like Alfred and what's-her-face. Jayne.

He pushed himself away from his car, fired his rag into a bucket and shoved it aside for the cleaning staff to deal with. Disgusted by the direction he'd allowed his thoughts to take, he decided to head for the house and take a long, cold shower. By the time he reached Cynthia's place, he hoped he'd be frozen to the core.

Heart included.

As she waited for Rick to pick her up for their fitting at The Phillip Michael Allen Wedding Boutique, Cynthia cuddled Rosy Cheeks and, with her jaw resting slack against her chest, read one of the love letters she'd found that morning among Alfred's attic effects. Her heart stalled and felt as if it had gone into a free fall as she studied the page she held and discovered not only the real reason Alfred had favored Cynthia, but also why he had left her everything.

Her eyes zipped over Jayne's now-familiar scrawl again, and then once again, just to be sure.

It had to be!

Excitement at having finally unfolded a puzzling mystery burned in her breast as she refocused her gaze and stared through the French doors to the fountain out back. There was no other explanation, now that she thought about it. After all, her credentials as a personal assistant had to be woefully short on qualifications. After she'd graduated high school, she'd given up her aspirations for college due to lack of finances. Yet Alfred had hired her, sight unseen, and transported her, lock, stock and dog, from Minnesota to Seattle to work for him as a personal assistant. She'd been too naive to wonder why.

Her gaze snapped back to the yellowed stationery and the words Jayne had written.

Alfred, please don't be angry. My parents told me that you'd been killed in action. You can only imagine my despair when I discovered they'd lied and you were still alive. Now I have no choice but to stay with Thomas, as we are expecting our first child.... You must understand I have to put the child first...our families have launched a business endeavor...will always love you. With all my heart...

There was more, but Cynthia's eyes were swimming in tears. The letter was postmarked Duluth, Minnesota, 1946. The year Cynthia's father had been born.

But even more important, the previous letters had been signed simply "Jayne," no return address. This one was signed by one Jayne Marie Coleman-*Noble*, wife of the dour "Duke" Thomas Noble.

And the eventual mother of William Noble, who would be...Cynthia's father.

Alfred's Jayne had been Cynthia's grandmother.

Thoughts swirled like bubbles down a bathtub drain.

Grandmother Jayne and Grandfather Duke hadn't been born married? Grandmother Jayne, so stern and proper, was once madly in love with the—Cynthia glanced at an old photo she held—*studly Alfred?*

The very thought was mind-boggling.

Now myriad comments made by Alfred in his dying days suddenly made sense.

You remind me so much of her. Mannerisms, your smile. The way you laugh.

Cynthia pulled a face as she remembered her grandmother's hoity-toity airs. Had she really reminded Alfred of her? *Bleech.* Maybe Jayne had been a bit softer and friendlier back in the good old days. Her letters were certainly passionate enough.

Never would Cynthia have ever guessed that the Jayne of the letters was the same obsessive-compulsive Jayne who had raised her poor father. In fact, in retrospect, Cynthia almost believed that Alfred had been better off without his "Lady Jayne."

Then again, the curmudgeonly Grandpa Duke could have curdled even the freshest milk.

As Cynthia sat ruminating, she began to draw disturbing parallels between Jayne, Duke and Alfred and her own relationship with Graham and Rick.

If Jayne had married Alfred instead of Duke, would she have been nicer? Less of a domineering perfectionist?

Then again, if the fates had allowed and Alfred had married her grandmother, neither she nor Rick would be here. They'd be other people.

Other, related people.

"You didn't have to do this."

Cynthia was referring not only to the ride to The Phillip Michael Allen Wedding Boutique, but to the actual tuxedo fitting, as well.

"Sure I did. After all, that's what brothers are for, right?"

She rolled her eyes away from Rick's handsome profile and jerked the seat belt across her lap. "Mmm-hmm. Right."

"We'd better put the pedal to the metal if we're going to make it there on time." Rick punched the accelerator, pinning her back against her seat as they flew down Alfred's drive.

"I'd be happy with late and alive."

"Oh, c'mon. I thought you liked living on the edge."

"Whatever gave you that absurd idea?"

"You're engaged to Graham, aren't you?"

Mouth clenched, she would not give him the satisfaction of letting her terror show as they peeled around the corner and onto the highway proper. He knew damn good and well that she did not want this fitting. Yet, with more tenacity than the Secret Service, he'd agreed to escort her every move that day. She bristled at his smug expression, knowing that he believed the more time he spent with her, the closer he'd get to the truth.

Whatever that was.

She wasn't sure herself anymore.

She knew only one thing. Her feelings for Rick Wingate were getting out of hand. Regardless of the fact that there wasn't much hope for a pseudoengaged woman and a man who thought she was a swindler, she'd allowed herself to dream.

Last night she'd had a terrible time falling asleep, for reliving that kiss. It had been pure magic. And as tough as he liked to act, she had to wonder if Rick hadn't felt the same way. Yes, he was out to prove something about her sham of an engagement, but she'd sensed something happening between them that went far beyond his quest for information.

One wrist draped casually over the steering wheel of his

Mercedes, he passed a truck whose spray assaulted the windshield with the force of a fire hose.

Cynthia twisted her fingers in her lap and began to recite the serenity prayer.

Rick didn't seem to notice. "So. What have you been up to lately?"

For a moment Cynthia debated. She didn't really want to confide in him. To share any more intimate moments. But on the other hand, she was dying to tell someone what she'd learned.

"I read."

"Letters?"

"Mmm-hmm."

"What did you find?"

She told him. Every heartbreaking detail.

Rick was unusually silent as she read to him from one of the letters that she'd tucked into her purse—along with Alfred's musty journal—when he'd arrived to pick her up that morning.

When she finished, he exhaled long and slowly.

"Your *grandmother* was the woman Alfred built the house for?" Eyes off the road, he looked at her in amazement.

"Rick! Please! Watch the road!"

He rolled his gaze at the sunroof. "Who's driving, you or me?"

"Apparently me, since I'm the only one in the car with my eyes on the road!"

"And you're doing a great job. We haven't crashed yet." With a languid grin, he directed his gaze back out the window. "Are you going to tell my parents?"

"When I get a moment to sit down with them uninterrupted, yes." She'd decided to wait until Graham was home and they could sort everything out together with Katherine and Harrison. Just another in the long list of blows his parents would suffer at her hands. Soon enough, poor Harrison would discover that his mother had not been his father's true love. Oh, yeah. She couldn't wait to deal that card.

"Wow. So that's why he left that monster of a house to you. You reminded him of her."

"Mmm-hmm, although I think his memories of her were somewhat...rosy."

"What makes you say that?"

"As I recall, Grandmother Jayne...wasn't all that nice, actually. I think Alfred might have been better off without her."

"Really?"

"She was a bit of a shrew, as I recall."

He threw back his head and laughed. "So she *was* just like you."

"Very funny. Now, would you please keep your eyes on the road before you get us both *killed?*"

"Yes, Jayne."

"Cute. Very cute."

Chapter Seven

"So she turned him down."

"No. Her father did." Cynthia's finger traced Alfred's scrawl to the top of the last page in his personal journal as they wound their way through the streets of downtown Seattle toward the wedding boutique. "Says here that he spent his last dime on musicians and some kind of special wine she liked and nearly a dozen roses. I guess he couldn't afford all twelve."

"Bummer."

"Then he went to her place and, on bended knee, begged her to run away with him. In the middle of his love song her father took a potshot. The wine bottle exploded, musicians and roses scattered and that was the end."

"Wow."

"Yeah." Cynthia sighed. "He pasted the song he wrote for her to the back cover of this book." She flipped the page and squinted at the yellowed words. Small instructions under the title "Lady Jayne" directed the performer to "Sing to the tune of 'Take Me Out to the Ball Game.'"

She gnawed the inside of her cheek and frowned. That was hardly a romance classic. Curious, she half read, half sang aloud.

"'My...'"

She cleared her throat and began again.

"'My dearest Jayne, loneliness is my bane. I'm like a crooked cane—'" Cynthia squinted. Yes, it actually said that. "Or a small Great Dane, something profane, without the gain of my lady Jayne—'"

Rick groaned and Cynthia watched his face scrunch with unbridled laughter. She battled back a rude guffaw of her own and attempted to continue, although how this fit the tune was a bit of a puzzler.

"'Out here on the lane of Oak and Main, I'm in pain, as it's starting to rain, oh my laaaadeeey Jayne!'"

Rick's laughter was the snorting variety now. His eyes were scrunched tightly shut, and again Cynthia had to wonder how he knew where he was driving. Never mind. She was too giddy to care. Besides, they hadn't crashed yet. Her own laughter bubbling now, Cynthia gave up and simply read.

"'Yes, I'm insane, my lady Jayne, don't let me love in vain, please don't let our love wane...oh, it's one, two, three kisses for you, if you'll marry me....'"

By now they were howling.

For several blocks their rollicking hoots filled the car as they spurred each other to thigh-slapping hilarity.

"'Ohhhhh'" they sang at the top of their lungs, "'it's *one, two, three* kisses for you, if you'll marrrrry meeeee....'"

Rick gasped and wiped his eyes. "Okay, then. I can now see why her father tried to shoot him."

Cynthia clutched her middle and slapped at him to stop.

But he was on a hilarity roll. "Come to think of it—" he panted between fits "—back when we were kids he'd pen an endless ode now and again for the holidays. We were told we couldn't open our presents until he finished. Yes, it was a festive torture, usually set to the tune of some poor hymn. 'Oh, come all ye turkeys and joyful giblet gravy…''' Cynthia screamed with glee at that. "They *never* made sense…one after the other…on and on…"

Again they fell silent with belly-grabbing laughter.

"Hey, now. We're not being very nice." Cynthia fished in her pockets for a tissue to dab her leaking orifices. "I think it's sweet. Yes, I'll admit he was no poet, and it does appear as if he combed the alphabet for words that rhymed with Jayne, but still, he was trying, and I have to admire that."

Their laughter finally waned to the occasional chuckle. Rick glanced at Cynthia. "Graham write you poetry?"

"No."

"Mmm."

"Oh, and I suppose you're a veritable Longfellow." She giggled.

"I could do better than that." He inclined his head toward the book she held in her hands as his eyes scanned the storefronts that passed before them.

"I'd like to see you try," she taunted.

"I would, my dear, but—" he cranked the wheel and pulled into a rare vacant parking spot on the street in front of a very upscale wedding boutique "—we're here."

They both grinned at his silly rhyme.

"You must be the happy couple."

Phillip Michael Allen looked anything but.

"Actually, we're—"

"Actually, you're *late*." His accusatory squint had both Rick and Cynthia groping for words.

"I told you," Rick whispered behind his hand.

"Five minutes. Big deal," she whispered back.

With tentative steps they entered the high-tech boutique and sent apprehensive glances at the stark black walls and overabundance of mirrors. Their reflections were multiplied like that of a dumbstruck chorus line. The atmosphere was so somber, Rick had to wonder if they hadn't stumbled into a mortuary by mistake.

"Well, come on. Don't just stand there gaping at me. I'll give you the remaining twenty-five minutes of my precious time, and then you're on your own." Two sharp claps brought his entourage scurrying as he spun and sashayed across the gleaming hardwood floor to the racks that he and his staff had prepared for their meeting.

"Twenty-five *minutes?* Twenty-five *seconds* is far too long with this clown," Rick muttered, grabbing Cynthia by the arm and pulling. "C'mon. Let's get out of here."

"As I recall, it was your idea to come with me," she groused under her breath, and jerked her arm from his grasp. "So, *you* come on. Marcella is counting on us." Stepping behind him, she planted her hands at his back and pushed.

A reluctant grin tipped his lips and, obliging, Rick shuffled across the floor. "Can't disappoint Marcella."

"You have a thing for Marcella?" she teased.

"Shut up. She could be your sister-in-law," he tossed over his shoulder.

"Yes, but you'd have to kiss her."

"Jealous?"

"No. *I* don't want to kiss her!"

"Can't blame you there." They giggled like recalcitrant schoolkids.

"Colors?" Phillip Michael snapped a look over his shoulder and pinned Rick and Cynthia with his piercing gaze.

Everyone—including the entourage—froze.

Over Rick's shoulder, he and Cynthia exchanged puzzled glances.

Phillip Michael was forced to repeat himself, something he did not often deign to do. Shoulders dropping with impatience at their complete and total lack of nuptial competence, he spoke slowly, as if educating a pair of simpletons. "What…colors…will…you…be using…in…your…wedding?"

"Uh…" Rattled, Cynthia slipped her hand into Rick's and held tight. "I…"

"We like…" Rick took a protective step between Cynthia and Phillip Michael and noted that she was wearing a sunny orange-and-yellow T-shirt and a yellow fleece jacket. "Lemon? And…uh, orange? The, uh, fruit range, I guess you could say."

Cynthia stared at him and mouthed, *The fruit range?*

Rick shrugged and grinned.

No comment was necessary as Phillip Michael's puckered lips spoke volumes.

"You," Phillip Michael barked at Rick. "Hubby!"

"Actually, I—"

"You first." With a practiced glance Phillip Michael sized him up. "Forty-two long. Get him that Armani we just got in, with an eggplant cummerbund. Your wedding colors have just changed, please make a note of it." He spun to look Cynthia up and down and this time clapped thrice. "Halston! Karan! Von Furstenberg! She's a six. Nnooo, eight."

Belatedly Cynthia sucked in her stomach.

Phillip Michael's entourage sprang into action. Soon dressing rooms were laden with tuxedos and flowing gowns and Cynthia and Rick were instructed to go their separate ways and strip.

A wall-size mirrored partition kept them from seeing one another, but Rick could hear the rustling of fabric and the breathless murmurs of Cynthia's assistants as she tried on a number of dresses. As for himself, he had two very hairless, space-age Euro-Dieter types in horn-rimmed glasses, black turtlenecks and pants tucked into black motorcycle boots pushing, prodding, buttoning and zipping him into his tux.

"Goot." One nodded at the finished product and brushed nonexistent lint from Rick's shoulders.

"Ya. Is *goot*, ya." His partner agreed with seesawing brows.

Rick glanced in the mirror at their approving faces, then gave himself a once-over and had to admit he did look rather snappy. There wasn't much need for a tux in his line of work, so the transformation from jeans to this was drastic. He'd need a haircut and a shave, of course. And he would have to lose the hoop in his ear, as that wasn't exactly formal....

As he fingered his earlobe, reality struck and he gave his head a sharp shake. What on earth was he thinking? He wasn't the groom. This wasn't his tux. There was no reason to shave, or get a haircut, or even show up at the wedding, for that matter.

"Not goot?" One of the Dieters was concerned by the sudden scowl on Rick's face.

Rick exhaled. "No, no, it's...fine. Really."

"Goot."

"People!" Phillip Michael's abrupt voice startled them from over the intercom. "Code aquamarine. Our next clients have arrived and they are *early*. Stations, please. Prepare Salon B."

The entourage vaporized like a summer mist, leaving Rick and Cynthia alone in their dressing areas. Wondering what to do next, Rick pushed his jacket aside and slipped his hands into his pockets. Whistling under his breath, he read the emergency evacuation card, pulled at a thread in his shirt and tried to stop thinking about Cynthia, in whatever state of undress, just behind the mirror.

The diversionary tactics were not effective.

"Cynthia?" he whispered.

Her tentative response reached him from behind the mirror. "Yeah?"

"I just wondered... I don't know. What you were doing."

"Not much. How do you look?"

"Formal," he replied. "How about you?"

Silence.

"What, no comment?"

Louder silence.

"Oh, c'mon. It can't be that bad." Curiosity got the better of him and he stepped to the mirror and, craning his neck around the partition's corner, took a peek.

And what he saw there squeezed the oxygen from his lungs.

She was so *beautiful*.

Blood roared, like the ocean's surf, in his ears, and his mouth went hot-sandy-beach dry. From the long train of her dress to the gentle swell of her hips, and from the myriad buttons that cinched the bodice at her waist to the back of her delicate neck she was stunning. Her hair was upswept and held loosely with a clip, and when his gaze moved to the reflection of her face, he could see tears swimming in her eyes. Tears?

Several steps carried him to her side of the dressing area, and he bent to take a closer look at the streaks on her mottled cheeks. "What's wrong?" Gently he brushed at them with the backs of his knuckles.

Sniffs and hiccups accompanied her watery smile. "Oh, I, well, it's just..." She shrugged. "It's just that this is how I always imagined it would be. Like a fairy princess.

But I also imagined that—'' She swiped at a tear with the edge of her hand. "Oh, nothing."

"What? You imagined what?"

"I imagined that my...my...you know...true love would be here with me."

"And he can't be here."

"No. He can't be *with* me."

The muscles in Rick's jaw jumped. Where the hell was Graham? What kind of a man could skip off to another country and leave such a beautiful woman right before his wedding? Graham didn't deserve her. For pity's sake, *he* seemed to care a helluva lot more about Cynthia than Graham ever did. A whole helluva lot more. Far more than he had a right to, in fact.

"I'm sorry," he murmured, wishing he could make it better.

Palms flat against her skirts, Cynthia ducked her head and smoothed the folds. "It's okay. This will all work out. Eventually."

"If it's any consolation, you look—" he had to clear his throat to disguise the catch in his voice "—really beautiful."

Her head snapped up. "You think?"

"Oh, yeah."

Their gazes met in the mirror, and Rick watched his arm rise and settle at Cynthia's waist. Together they made the model couple for the top of a cake.

"Thank you. You're not so bad yourself."

"I need a haircut."

"*No!* I mean, not really." Embarrassment tinged her cheeks. "I like your hair just as it is. Short hair wouldn't suit you."

A flurry of movement from behind had them refocus as Phillip Michael and his many assistants swept into their dressing area. Upon spying the two of them standing together, he stopped and stared, aghast.

"What in the *name* of *holy matrimony* are the two of you *doing?*" Assuming a posturing snit, he threw his hands up in disgust. "Don't you know that to *see* each other before the wedding in your *dress* and *tux* is the kiss of *death?*"

Expressions equally agog, the entourage looked from Phillip Michael to Rick and Cynthia and back to Phillip Michael.

"Well, never mind. It's sure as hell too late now. You might as well say your 'I do's' and get it over with. Although—" Circling his chin with his thumb and forefinger, he gave his head a thoughtful nod and slowly strolled around the pair. "Mmm, mmm, mmm. I do have to say you make a drop-dead-gorgeous couple. It's the clothes."

The entourage nodded.

Rick saw the heat blotch Cynthia's creamy cleavage, then travel up her neck and to her cheeks.

"But we're not—"

With a flip of his hands, Phillip Michael ignored Rick and ordered, "Kiss your bride. Give us a thrill."

"But she's—"

"Go on," the fashion fussbudget barked, and glanced in irritation at his watch. "Kiss her, man. What's wrong with you?"

Rick and Cynthia laughed the nervous laughter of those put into a situation of extreme discomfort.

Thinking they were about to capitulate and share a little kiss, the entourage broke into huge smiles and waited with an expectation that was palpable.

Nobody moved.

Including Rick and Cynthia.

The silence grew heavy. The anticipation increased in intensity. Cynthia giggled at her shoes. Rick chuckled at the ceiling. People began sending covert glances amongst themselves, brows lifted with curiosity.

Phillip Michael gave his throat a noisy clearing. "Listen, man. We don't have the rest of our lives here. Kiss her, already. What is with you people, making us wait all day for everything?"

Dropping his shoulders, Rick fixed Phillip Michael with a challenging stare. If it was a show he wanted, then by golly, it was a show he'd get.

Slipping his arms around Cynthia's waist, he hauled her up against his chest. Everyone else's intake of air echoed her own and the room went silent for lack of breathing. Arms dangling, eyes flashing, toes tipping and lips oh-so-dewy, she stared up at him, and Rick was suddenly not quite so confident.

After yesterday's edict that he stay away from her, he had to wonder how she'd react. He was risking a slap in the face here, but he didn't really care. It was too late. Way, way, way too late.

For them all.

There was no stopping what Phillip Michael had just set into motion. So, that being the case, Rick ran the palm of one hand up the bodice of her dress, over the smooth hills of her bare shoulder blades and up to the clip in her hair, which came out with a single tug. Set free, her hair tumbled down about her shoulders.

So far, no signs of struggle on her part.

He wound his fist into the silken tresses and used it to angle her mouth under his.

When his lips slowly met hers, the sigh in the room was unanimous. For a moment they hovered like that, his lips just barely touching hers, breathing each other's breath, questioning, wondering if she really meant what she'd said yesterday. Though she'd been right about them staying away from each other, it was proving to be a virtual impossibility.

Rick lingered, not pressing, and then the tiniest arch of her body toward him was all it took to communicate her willing—if not all the way thought out—participation. Her arms slipped around his waist and she splayed her hands at his back. A step to the side on his part allowed her to move between his legs and he was able to pull her closer still.

And that was when it happened.

As his mouth gently prodded hers—so warm and supple and inviting—into submission, Rick lost his heart to Cynthia. Forever. And in her answering kiss he could sense the same thing happening within her own heart.

Rick felt as if the floor had fallen out from under his feet. He was weightless. Electrified. Lost.

And he never, ever wanted to find his way back from this feeling of perfect bliss. Warm and soft and at the same time hot and rough, the kiss continued, changing, permuting, becoming a vehicle through which they could let each other know their true feelings.

This kiss was far too pure to be a lie. Everything about it was real, from the way she clung to him, breath labored, heart pounding, hands clutching, to the way she stared at him through heavy-lidded eyes when he paused to change the angle of their mouths.

It went on this way for some time before a nervous chuckle issued from the entourage.

"Looks like they're gonna live happily ever after," Phillip Michael deadpanned.

The laughter spread, finally penetrating Rick's muzzy brain. Slowly he lifted his lips from Cynthia's and, still breathing like a pair of giant coal bellows, looked at her in confusion.

How could this be? He'd found her. His soul mate. The one he'd been looking for his whole life.

And she was his brother's woman.

Sick at his habitual betrayal of not only Graham and Cynthia, but of his own moral code, he stared at her with a horrible regret and whispered, "I'm sorry. I didn't mean to—"

"Just…" She planted her hands against his chest and pushed. "Don't."

Reading the distress on her face as guilt, Rick tried to pull her back and convince her that this was not her fault.

"Don't," she repeated again, this time more sharply.

Immediately he dropped his hands.

Face twisted with anxiety, Cynthia turned and rushed into the privacy of the dressing room, leaving everyone to wonder what had just happened.

Rick licked his lips and turned to address the curious crowd. "Uhh, she's…uh, she's my brother's fiancée."

"Ahhhh." Phillip Michael nodded as if that explained everything.

"Cynthia?"

Head bowed into her hands, Cynthia sat on a hard wooden bench in the dressing room and listened to Rick's soft voice filter though the door's crack.

"Cynthia, are you all right?"

Well, now, there was a question. She was in love with Graham's brother. Was that all right?

"Oh, I'm okay." With great difficulty she kept the tears out of her voice. Her gaze focused on the French-chiffon-and-lace skirts of the beautiful wedding gown she wore. Absently she plucked at the intricate pearl beadwork, hand detailed at her bodice, and wondered if she could wear this getup to school, being that it would cost her two years' clothing budget. "I'm just having a hard time unbuttoning all these thousands of tiny buttons without three hands and a buttonhook.''

"Ah. Well, listen. Everyone went to go help that other couple, so it's just you and me back here now. Why don't you let me in, and I'll help you get unbuttoned.''

Cynthia peered through her fingers at her side of the door with bleary eyes. "I don't think that would be such a good idea." She sniffed.

Rick cleared his throat. "Well, we can't stay here all day. Phillip Michael would kill us for going overtime.'' His attempt at levity fell flat. "I promise to be a good boy.''

Yes, but could she promise to be a good girl? She was still burning with humiliation at the way she'd so wholeheartedly thrown herself into that kiss back there. It was as if she'd actually believed this was her wedding and she was kissing the man she'd spend the rest of her life with.

And it had felt so right.

In that single kiss she'd found the other half of herself. Not to mention a very real sense of family when she imagined coming into the Wingate clan through Rick.

All her life she'd listened to her friends wax poetic about falling in love, and all her life she'd wondered at this great mystery. They'd all seemed so giddy and scatterbrained—and idiotic, truth be told—upon meeting Mr. Right. And she? When she'd met Graham, there were none of the fireworks her friends had described. Through all of the engagement hullabaloo, her feet were planted firmly on the ground. She'd proudly chalked this up to being levelheaded. She was secure in the knowledge of her future. As far as euphoria went, it had only ever reached the stage of a pleasant sense of belonging.

And even that had begun to wane when Alfred died.

But now?

Oh, have mercy, now that she'd experienced rapture in

Rick's arms, she could fathom all the hidden nuances behind the meaning of life. The veritable mysteries of the universe. Now she even understood the convoluted meaning of the saddest of country-and-western lyrics. She—

"Cynthia? Are you going to let me in?"

Jerking to attention, she swiped at her eyes and dabbed at her cheeks with the handy box of tissues left in the dressing room, compliments of Phillip Michael Allen. What choice did she have?

Voice feeble, she capitulated. "Yes. You can come in."

He jiggled the knob, to discover it locked. "Uh, Cynthia?"

Oh. Right. Listlessly she battled her skirts until she was able to stand and slog to the door. Pushing it open, she slowly lifted her gaze from the satiny tips of her shoes to the liquid pools of his eyes.

And she was lost all over again.

Her breathing became shallow, her head light and her pulse thready. Just like all of her giddiotic girlfriends from high school.

Rick pushed past her into the dressing room and closed the door behind him. Quarters were close as they turned and warily surveyed each other.

Smooth as chocolate thunder, Rick's voice rolled low into her ear. "Turn around and I'll unbutton you."

Without a word, she acquiesced. They stood facing the mirror and Cynthia watched him focus on this fiddly task as he spoke. "I'm sorry about that kiss. It was all my fault."

Another wound to the pile of barbecue beef that posed as her heart. "Please stop. You don't have to apologize to me again." She met his brief glance in the mirror and the lift of her brow reminded him of the kiss they'd shared— and that he'd apologized for—back in Alfred's attic.

"Oh." He nodded and went back to the buttons. "In

any event, I had no business taking advantage like that, even though we were goaded. So—" he cleared his throat and shrugged "—I'll agree to forget it, if you will."

Cynthia's eyes fell closed and she swallowed hard. He could forget that? Her stomach turned over. Never in a lifetime could she forget the beauty of that moment. But, being that he was Graham's brother, and not her fiancé, she could only nod.

As Rick's fingers blazed their way down her spine, she could feel his exhalation ruffle her hair. A sigh of relief, no doubt. He could drive her home and escape, once he'd sprung her from this dress. The bitter bile of unrequited love burned.

"Cynthia?" Something in his quiet tone had her suddenly straining to hear between the lines. "Before we forget what has happened between us entirely, I have to get one thing off my chest." He flicked open the last button at the base of her spine and his eyes met hers in the mirror. "I do not understand why Graham isn't here in this room with you right now. If I were your fiancé, I'd be here to plan every stage of our wedding. In fact, I'd never have left, no matter how important the business deal. Because if you can't put your family ahead of your business, then who are you?"

"The way you did when Alfred was dying?" She flung the words at him, her misery making her cruel.

Rick winced as she hit a sore spot. "You're right. But I learned something very important about priorities. It was a mistake I'll never repeat again."

Cynthia averted her eyes, ashamed that she'd lashed out at him when he so obviously cared. She wasn't used to such concern.

"Even so, Cynthia, this is different. Graham is your husband-to-be. Your life. Yet every time I've ever seen the two of you interact, it's with derision, and that worries

me." His fingers lingered on her back, leaving her bare
flesh exposed to his touch. He turned her around to better
search her face, and the scrutiny had her squirming.

"Kind of like us, huh?"

"No," he protested. "Not at all like…us."

She swallowed. She didn't want his worry.

"I just can't understand how he could leave you at all,
let alone on the heels of Alfred's death. And then, with
this wedding to plan? He's always been selfish, but this
goes beyond reason. Where the hell is he, Cynthia?"

"I can't…tell you."

"Why?" Rick's hand slid up her forearms and he
gripped her biceps in the palms of his hands and lightly
shook. *"Why?"*

Why indeed? She felt herself losing her ability to reason.
Again their breathing became hurried and shallow. Again
their bodies yearned for the forbidden. Again they struggled with reality.

"Because Graham…because he…" More than any-
thing, Cynthia wanted to confide in Rick. To tell him about
her breakup with Graham. To fall into his arms and spill
her true feelings. But she couldn't. Her word was her
creed, even if Graham's was not. Besides, telling Rick now
would seem opportunistic. As if the breakup had been
something convenient she'd concocted, so that she and
Rick could carry on behind Graham's back.

She'd promised to honor Graham's blasted parting request. And there were too many people involved at this
point to simply blurt out the truth. Katherine, Harrison,
Marcella and now Phillip Michael. Her head began to
throb just thinking of the thumping she'd get when this
whopper snowball finally mowed her over.

She could only hope that she was standing behind Graham when it hit.

"You know—" Abruptly Rick let go of her arms and,

dragging a hand over his face, took a step back. "I don't want to know. Whatever is going on between the two of you defies logic and is, frankly, none of my business." He slapped the door frame with the flat of his palm. "I'll meet you in the lobby after you've finished changing." And with that, he was gone.

Rick sat in his car and watched Cynthia disappear into Alfred's place, his mind vacillating with the rhythmic cadence of his windshield wipers. He had no business worrying about her now that she'd just slipped through the front door and triggered the alarm system. Beyond seeing her safely home, she was not his responsibility.

She was Graham's.

It was time for Rick to put his Mercedes into gear and head firmly back into his own life. Easier said, of course.

It was done. Pandora's box opened. That morning at Phillip Michael Allen's had put any questions about a mutual attraction between them to rest.

He wanted her.

And it was obvious that she felt the same.

But Graham had some kind of hold over her. And it wasn't love.

That being the case, how could he in good conscience allow this wedding to proceed?

His thoughts strayed to Graham, causing his fingers to flex on the steering wheel. Graham. His perennially selfish younger brother, on a working vacation in Europe. Rick would bet a hefty sum of money on the fact that Graham was enjoying the company of another woman at this very moment. And it was the middle of the night in Paris now....

Rick gazed at the lamp glowing in the window of Alfred's old suite, and the homey radiance took on the quality of flames in his mind's eye. Flames of anger toward Graham.

Wanting to burn some of his fury out of his system, Rick threw his car into gear and bore down the driveway, thinking that if Graham didn't show up soon, he was going to go hunt him down.

And what happened from there would have little to do with polite conversation.

Her spine curled against a pillow, Cynthia sat cross-legged on her bed with Rosy Cheeks in her lap. She watched from Alfred's old window as Rick's taillights grew dimmer until they finally disappeared into the northwest mist. Mouth turned down at the corners, heart heavy, she pushed her fingers through the dog's fur. Rosy Cheeks licked her hands, seeming to sense her pain.

"I blew it, girl," she murmured. "Went and fell in love with a man I can never have."

Rosy Cheeks whimpered and rolled on her back, exposing her belly for a good rub.

"Why, you ask? Why can I never have him? Well, for one thing, I was engaged to his brother first. Then I went and inherited the house his mother wanted, which—even though she's been so nice about it—hurt her terribly. Then I broke up with her little darling. Then, while everyone thinks I'm planning the wedding of the century to their baby, I go and have an affair, of sorts—even though Graham and I were broken up at the time, mind you—with his older brother."

Cynthia sighed and the dog's eyes seemed to bulge more than normal at this barrage of sin and iniquity.

"I'm scum." Cynthia scratched the dog's belly till her legs began to twitch. "Yes, bona fide scum. Alfred would be appalled. Perhaps the only one who would not be appalled would be my rather anarchic pseudofiancé."

She reached for the cordless phone on her nightstand. "Speaking of Graham, I think it's time for another call, don't you, Rosy Cheeks?"

Rosy Cheeks growled.

"Mmm. My sentiments exactly."

The phone rang as she held it in her hand. She frowned and pushed the talk button. "Hello?"

"Cynthia? Katherine here, dear. How was the fitting at Phillip Michael Allen's today?"

"The fitting? Oh, it was, golly, uh, it was so...so... words just can't—"

"Wonderful! Listen, darling. The reason I'm calling is to invite you out to dinner this coming Friday evening. Harrison and I have been researching restaurants for your rehearsal dinner and think we have it narrowed down to a select few. This one is at the top of my list and so I'll need your approval, as the dinner is fast approaching. Chez Moustache? You've heard of it?"

"I...uh, no."

"Never mind. You'll love it. Fabulous French cuisine, according to Marcella. You don't have to work, do you?"

"Uh, this Friday night? Umm...no. I'm not on the schedule."

"Wonderful. I'll have Rick pick you up at six-thirty."

"Oh, Katherine, that really won't be necessary! I can—"

"Now, Harrison and I are firm about not wanting you out at night in that old rattletrap car of yours. Okay, then, darling. Six-thirty, this Friday night."

And without further ado, Katherine rang off.

Chapter Eight

Chez Moustache was a charming French bistro, intimate yet large enough for the wedding party to party after the rehearsal, in less than a week. The three Wingates—Katherine, Harrison, Rick—and, unfortunately to her way of thinking, Cynthia were seated that Friday night at a cozy table near a window overlooking one of Seattle's many dazzling lakes. Christmas ships, like a floating wonderland, sailed slowly past, the parade of lights causing all patrons to ooh and aah. The dulcet tones of holiday music and low conversation underscored the festive feel. In the middle of the room a fire crackled in a giant fire pit and everywhere, decorations and lights twinkled, reminding one and all that it was the season to be…jolly.

And so far, Katherine was the jolliest.

Delighted with every detail, she commented on the fantastic service, the beautiful surroundings, the delicious food and the chic patronage. Her lively energy had her eyes sparkling and her cheeks flushed. Though Cynthia knew that both she and Rick had been reticent about attending this command performance, in their own ways neither of them could help enjoying Katherine's youthful enthusiasm. And Harrison? Well, Harrison hadn't stopped beaming for over two weeks now. Not since his wife had set the wedding plans into motion.

Though Cynthia tried to keep reality in sight throughout the evening, Katherine's head-in-the-clouds world was contagious. For them all. Again she and Rick seemed to forget that they needed to keep an emotional distance, and allowed themselves the pleasure of a night out together. The dinner conversation ebbed and flowed in the interesting and comfortable ways of family, and Cynthia relished the warm feeling of inclusion.

Until Phillip Michael Allen happened by their table.

"Wingate?" he inquired, just to make sure.

"Yes?" Face reflecting the season's happy glow, Katherine nodded.

"Phillip Michael Allen." He flopped his hand out to her, then Harrison for a pair of limp handshakes. "I'm doing the apparel for your son's wedding."

Eyes bugging, Cynthia glanced at Rick, who was suddenly struggling with the button at his collar.

"Well, isn't this a lovely coincidence!" Katherine gestured to an empty chair at a table behind them. "Won't you join us?"

Rick began to cough and Cynthia pounded him on the back.

"Oh, no, no, no. Thank you. Actually, my mother is waiting for me to join her for dinner. I just wanted to stop and tell you that you have one of the closest-knit families that I have ever seen."

The coughing and choking from Rick grew more worrisome and Cynthia handed him a glass of water.

"How sweet of you to say so." Delighted with the

praise, Katherine seemed not to notice her firstborn's struggle for oxygen.

"Yes." Phillip Michael pinned Rick with a shrewd look. "I've never met such a helpful brother. My staff and I will certainly never forget our most remarkable time spent together with your son and his...er—" he waved toward Cynthia "—uh, her, there." His head swiveled back to Katherine. "I'll have the dress and tux delivered Monday afternoon, as the alterations were slight. Tuesday morning at the very latest."

"Oh, thank you, Mr. Allen, for giving us your precious time and attention on such short notice."

"You're entirely welcome. And when you send out the invitations, please add me to the list, as I simply must see the final project."

"Oh!" Katherine gave Phillip Michael's hand a spritely little pat, then turned to beam at Cynthia and Rick. "Well, actually, the date has been set for a week from tomorrow. The day before Christmas Eve was the only time we could find where everyone would still be in town, if you can believe that."

"Can I? Listen, honey, I hear you. I'm crazy with entertaining, myself. Mother is here from Santa Fe and she expects to be treated like the Queen of Sheba—"

"Bring her with you to the wedding! Your invitation will be slightly late, as I sent everything out last week."

Inhaling sharply with shock, Cynthia also began to choke, and grabbed her water glass back from Rick. Somehow, in all the confusion, she hadn't remembered that they would actually be *inviting* people to this charade. She felt herself beginning to turn blue. Still struggling with his own spasms, Rick pounded her between the shoulder blades.

Not noticing their distress, Katherine burbled on. "Marcella advised that if I didn't do it first thing, what with the holidays coming, the mail would be slow and they never would have made it on time.''

''You—'' Another coughing fit had Cynthia's hands waving and her eyes tearing. ''You,'' she gasped at last, ''already *sent out* the invitations?''

''Of course, dear.'' Katherine's laughter tinkled. ''If you want any guests to attend this extravaganza, you need to invite them. Don't bother thanking me, honey. It was my pleasure. In fact,'' she confided to Phillip Michael, ''with any luck, they've already arrived.''

''Graham! She has already sent out the invitations!'' Cynthia wound the phone cord from the wall around her finger until it turned purple with pain.

Frightened by her master's voice, Rosy Cheeks leaped off the bed and scuttled out of the room.

''Cynthia, I can't believe you didn't see that coming.''

''I've been a little *busy!* Listen, buddy, allowing the wedding preparations to go this far was not part of our deal.'' After a number of tries that evening, Cynthia had finally located Graham in his Parisian hotel, at breakfast— Paris time—with a supposed client. ''You promised me last time we spoke that you'd try to come home!''

Impatience tinged his voice. ''And I will.''

''When?'' Cynthia took a moment to hold the phone out in front of her chest and squeeze, as if it were Graham's neck. ''When, Graham? I need dates. Times. *Flight numbers.*''

''I'm working on it.''

''Graham, our wedding is slated to happen this coming *Saturday morning, doves and all.* If you don't get your butt home and explain this mess to your family by... by...*tomorrow,* I'm telling everyone that we are not engaged and that you knew it all along but wouldn't let me tell. Then I'm going to promise to pay back every cent your parents have spent and *you're going to help me!*"

"*No.*"

"Yes!"

"Cynthia...don't." He sighed. "I know this is hard to believe, but I love my parents."

"So?"

Since his answer was not immediately forthcoming, Cynthia had to wonder exactly what he was up to. It was so hard to tell with Graham. Could he be lying to her now, the way he lied to everyone else? She plunged her fingertips through her hair, grabbed a handful at the crown and rested her nose against her bicep. Eyes tightly scrunched, she whispered, "If you love them so dearly, then how could you lie to them this way?"

"I..." He sighed. "I don't look at it as a lie."

Jaw sagging, Cynthia stopped pacing Alfred's Turkish rug and snapped her gaze to her reflection in the mirror. And she'd at one time thought him to be an honest and— even more naively—*rational* human being?

"Then—" she held a palm of supplication to the ceiling "—would you mind telling me how you *do* look at it?"

"Cynthia, you are the first fiancée I ever had that my parents truly loved. And because they love you so much, they seem to love me more."

Cynthia chewed her lower lip and listened intently.

"I've always been something of a disappointment to them, and growing up in the perfect Rick's shadow didn't help. But you changed all that for me. They are proud of me now. Because of you, I'm respectable."

Cynthia drew a deep breath through her nose and held it to a count of ten to prevent saying something she'd regret.

Graham, she realized for the first time since she'd met him, was even more of an orphan than she'd been. Though he'd grown up surrounded by family, he was dying for validation. As a boy, he'd been far too needy for ineffectual, self-absorbed parents like Katherine and Harrison. Instead of making him strong and independent, as it had Rick, it had sent him on an endless quest for approval. Approval that would never come until he learned to accept himself.

Unfortunately, Cynthia was not his ticket to respectability. To acceptance. To the conditional love that his parents were unaware they'd withheld when he didn't perform as expected.

Slowly she let her breath out through her lips. "Yes, but Graham, at what price are you getting your respectability? I...I...don't love you."

Graham was silent, and she pressed the cool plastic of the headpiece closer to her ear to at least hear his breathing. Over the lines that connected them from continent to continent came the faint strains of other conversations bleeding through, in other languages, on other lines. Conversations of business. Of joy. Of the mundane. Of starting over.

Cynthia hated that they were having this conversation on the phone. She couldn't see his eyes, and as much as he was a screwup in his personal life, he had a lot of good qualities. A lot of potential. She really had no desire to hurt his feelings.

"The love I feel for you is not like a wife," she amended softly. "More like a...sister."

"Isn't that enough?"

Exasperated, she slapped her forehead. "*No,* Graham! No! And you don't love me either, and you know it!"

"But my mother is happy. I'm the one who brought her out of her depression!"

"No, you're not!"

"Her happiness makes Dad happy, too. He's told me,

Cynthia. We've been talking on the phone. He's proud of me, hon. For the first time, he's really proud.''

"But Graham, don't you see that when they find out what you've done, your mother is going to be more depressed than ever? That your father will be disappointed?''

"Not if you marry me this Saturday.''

She smacked the receiver against the palm of her hand. Was this thing working? *"I'm not marrying you!"*

"We don't have to be in love to marry. I'll take care of you in style. You will never want for anything.''

Except love. Fidelity. Passion.

"No! A thousand times, no! Get that through your head! Come home now, and tell your mother. Or I will.''

Graham was silent for a full, torturous minute. "All right,'' he finally snapped. "I'll call with flight information as soon as possible. In the meantime, don't say a word to my mother or my father. Criminy, Cynthia. You inherit the house from the old man. The least you can do is wait a few more days before breaking my mother's heart. Again.''

Cynthia pitched face first onto the comforter at the end of Alfred's bed and groaned as he continued his emotional blackmail.

"This whole thing is going to humiliate my family.''

"And whose fault is that?''

"I'll assume part of the responsibility, yes.''

"Only *part?*''

"I'm living up to *my* part in this engagement commitment.''

Cynthia could only emit a guttural gasp at his delusion as she thought back to the lipstick on his chin at the funeral.

"Anyway,'' Graham continued, "before we drop this bomb, at least let me be there to support them.''

"Fine. Be a hero.'' She sat up and pushed her hair away

from her face. "The wedding is all set now, for Saturday.
If you don't want to be left at the altar—and don't think
I won't—be home before the wedding begins and *break
up with me! Publicly!*"

As she crashed the phone back into its cradle and
flopped back onto the bed, she could only hope that for
once, Graham would stick to his word.

The following days crawled by in a flurry of fallacious
wedding preparations and an eternal wait for Graham to
walk through the door.

Which he didn't.

Problems finding a flight seemed to plague him. That,
and an endless list of business dealings he claimed needed
to be handled, all at the last minute.

It was now already Wednesday. The rehearsal and dinner were scheduled for Friday. The wedding for Saturday.
The honeymoon for Sunday.

The loony bin for Monday.

Cynthia tried to keep her mind occupied by sorting
through Alfred's multitudinous closets, armoires, trunks
and boxes and the last of the letters, journals, newspaper
articles and other myriad documentation of his life. And
Tiffany—when she wasn't taking care of her son, or working at Pudgie's, or out with friends—had taken to helping
out.

Together that afternoon, Cynthia and the young girl
were in the attic, poring over Alfred's life, dissecting and
comparing his problems to their own.

"So." Tiffany, wearing one of Alfred's old military
jackets, paused in her sortings to rescue an old photo from
Hondo's sticky hands. "You're telling me that you are *still*
getting ready for a wedding? I thought you broke up with
squid-boy."

Seated cross-legged on the floor, Cynthia dropped her head into her hands and groaned. "I did."

"Then why the bogus wedding?"

"It's…it's…a long, convoluted story, but suffice it to say that Graham couldn't hurt his mother by telling her that we'd broken up. She was all depressed over Alfred's death and she's not a strong woman to begin with. Plus, Graham has been engaged a number of times before and they all fell through, so she really had high hopes for us. And because Graham is a mama's boy, and needs her constant approval, I'm picking out china that I don't need." Elbows to knees, Cynthia peered at the girl from between her fingers. "And since I'm an incurable people pleaser and can't seem to say no and risk hurting anyone—which stems from my earlier foster-care days, I think, but would need further analysis to be completely sure—I'm making a huge, hurtful mess…."

Tiffany nodded sagely. "Yeah. I hear that. Same thing happened to me with Hondo's daddy."

"It did?"

"Mmm-hmm. We were supposed to get married before Hondo was born, but Monk got a new girlfriend, and he didn't want his mother to know, so we planned this little wedding, and I got the dress and everything, but he ran off and his mother kicked me and Hondo out. And my mom doesn't want us…." She gazed at her little son with adoration. "I sure hope I'm never such a jackass to my kid."

Cynthia could feel her grin bloom in the palm of her hand. "You won't be. Someday you'll meet Prince Charming and you'll all live happily ever after."

"Like you?"

"Me?"

"Ricky-boy?"

"No!" Her palm grew warm from the sudden flush in her cheeks.

"Hey, Ricky, he's so fine, he's so fine I've lost my mind, hey, Ricky!"

"No!" Cynthia laughed. "How do you know that old song?"

"Mom used to play it real loud, when I was a baby. And stop changing the subject. You guys are in love. Everyone knows it." Tiffany held up a package of Alfred's love letters that Cynthia had given her to read. "Don't do like that buzz-kill Jayne and throw away a perfectly good man, just because everyone's telling you to do something else."

"Kind of like you. And Josh. And Trent?"

"Not!" Tiffany snorted at that. "Oh, that reminds me!" With a quick glance at her watch, she scrambled to her feet and tugged her pant legs back down around her boots. "Can you Hondo-sit for me for a little while this afternoon?"

"Again? Tiffany, I'm—" Cynthia rubbed her face, leaving a black streak on her forehead and cheeks "—terrible with babies. Every time you leave, he pitches a bloody fit. I think he hates me." She eyed Hondo, who was currently attempting to scale one of the support beams in the attic's knee wall.

Tiffany's voice took on a pleading quality. "No, he loves you. He told me."

"He can't talk." Mentally Cynthia heard the toilet flushing on her Spanish and Japanese homework assignments. She might as well face the fact that she was never going to get anything done without some serious peace and quiet.

It was the peace part she was having such trouble with, and it didn't help knowing that her troubles were all her fault. She couldn't blame Graham for being weak. She'd always known who he was, but had managed to overlook his faults, for Alfred's sake. For the sake of gaining a family.

At least through this ordeal she'd learned that honesty and integrity were worth far more than anyone's temporary happiness. Come January first, she was turning over a new leaf. Making a resolution.

Honesty at all costs.

Even if it hurt someone's feelings.

Cynthia sighed. Honestly, she did not feel like sitting with Hondo. But it wasn't yet the first of the year, either. She groaned as she watched Hondo roll off the support beam and bang his head. The ensuing shrieks worked directly to contract the muscles in her neck and jaw.

Tiffany picked up her son and bounced him about.

"Cynthia, I'm going wacky. I really need to get out and Christmas shop for him, without dragging him out from under the racks. I hate to ask, but there's totally no one else."

Cynthia's eyes slid shut. Those words. She knew them so well. These were the echoes of her own childhood, and again she had to wonder why there was never anyone else.

Unless, of course, you wanted to be left alone, and then there they were. Plaguing you. Making you think crazy thoughts. Unbidden, visions of Rick popped into her head. With a long puff she blew at the strands of hair that had come loose from her ponytail. She had to get him out of her system.

Figuring little Hondo would at least keep her distracted while she waited for Graham to show up, she gave her head a tired bob. "Okay."

Coltish legs leaping, Tiffany squealed with joy. "Oh, thank you, thank you, thank you. I'll be at the mall. Page me if you need me."

"It's dark already. Who will take you?"

"Trent has wheels. He should be here any sec."

"Trent?" Even Cynthia could hear the disgust in her voice. "You'd already made arrangements?"

From the driveway, a horn blared.

"I figured you'd say yes. That's Trent. Gotta go."

"Be back by nine—" The girl had already pounded halfway out the door and Cynthia had to holler to be heard, "Okay? Not a second later, or I'll worry!"

"Okay! And Cynthia?"

"Yeah?"

"Love you."

Cynthia grinned.

Until she saw Hondo's lip begin to quiver. Uh-oh. He stared after his mother, then up at Cynthia, and the tears began to spurt. Within seconds he'd cranked up the volume to a window-rattling decibel level.

"Hey, Hondo. She'll be back. Don't worry. Please, don't cry. Hmm…I bet you are either hungry, or, uh, sleepy, or…uh…wet. So. Since you can't tell me, let's try the process of deduction."

Tired beyond her years—and dreaming of a honeymoon in the Bahamas without Graham—Cynthia endured Hondo's wrath on her way to the kitchen. Once there, she opened the nearly empty refrigerator. Wow. They needed to go shopping. This was ridiculous. She surveyed the wilted carrots in the bottom drawer and wished once again that she hadn't let the staff go in such a hasty manner. Clearly, they'd been eating too many meals at Pudgie's.

"Milk, milk, milk," she muttered as Hondo wailed. "No milk. How could we already be out of milk?" She rummaged in the cabinets. "Hmm. How do you like powdered milk? I bet you do."

Hondo stared.

"Okay. Let's try it."

Balancing the child on her hip, Cynthia read the instructions on the box. After mixing the milk, she poured it into a sippy cup and beamed at the baby. "Mmm! Yummy! Try it. You'll like it. Look, it's good. See, Aunt Cynthia loves it." She pretended to drink.

Hondo didn't buy it.

"You see through my act? Okay." Cynthia took a slug and bit back the urge to rush to the sink and spit. *Awful* stuff. "Yum! Here." She held the cup up to Hondo's lips. "You try."

Hondo screamed and slapped the cup to the floor.

"Alllll righty, then. Not hungry. Let's see if you're wet?"

When they got to Tiffany's room she laid the small boy on the bed and with reluctant fingertips carried his soiled diaper to the trash. Back at the bed, she wiped him up to the best of her ability, then to cover any mistakes, liberally dashed his bottom with talc.

"Ohhh-kay." Cynthia paused to study the cloth diaper and the safety pins with the duckies on the tops. "You'll have to bear with me here, as I've never done this kind of diaper before. I'm a paper diaper kind of gal and…uh… hmm…this is kind of tricky…."

Hondo's sudden bug-eyed silence was a bad sign. His face flushed bright red. His body went stiff. His mouth would take a screwdriver to straighten out.

Cynthia frowned. Something was wrong. The way he was inhaling, so long and slow and… The child exhaled with a scream that crossed her eyes. His legs flailed, and she ducked and battled her way into the fray to discover that there was a spot of blood on his silky-smooth tummy.

She'd stuck him with a ducky pin.

Horrified, she grabbed the thrashing, shrieking, gasping, outraged child to her chest and sank to the edge of the bed. "Oh, honey! I'm so sorry. Oh, please forgive me. Shhh, oh, hush, please." She glanced about, sure that the cops would soon be bursting through the door to arrest her for attempted murder.

"Why don't we put on some pajamas and go nigh-nigh, okay?"

Frantic now, she laid him on the bed and tried to get his shirt off over his head. Impossibly, his crying increased in volume. Gracious. His head was huge. And the neck on this little T-shirt was so tiny. What the…? Beads of sweat broke out on her upper lip. "Hang on, honey. Aunt Cynthia is…trying to…" Her back was killing her as she hunched over the child and struggled to free him from this yellow cotton death trap.

It would be fair to say that once Hondo could no longer see his surroundings, he began to freak in earnest. Cynthia grew hot and panicky.

Scissors. That's what she needed. She would have to cut him out of this stupid outfit. She was going to write a scathing letter to the people who manufactured such dangerous baby apparel!

The phone rang, further jangling her nerves. *Dammit!* It had better be a paramedic.

"Hello?" she barked, and thrust the wireless unit between her chin and shoulder, where it slithered about as she worked. Hondo's rage didn't help.

"Cynthia?"

"I'm sorry. You're going to have to speak up. It's a little noisy in here." She grabbed a fresh diaper, wiped her eyes and nose, then pulled down the little T-shirt and tackled Hondo's. Hondo didn't like that and let her know by creating an impromptu waterfall on Tiffany's bed.

Cynthia screamed.

"Cynthia? It's Rick. What's wrong?"

"Everything," she wailed. "Nothing. I don't know. I'm not good at this."

"At what?"

"At...children!" She sobbed for a moment before she could pull herself together enough to explain. "I think he's trapped...and he's...bleeding and it's all my fault!"

"Hang on. I'll be right there."

"No! I don't want you—"

Dial tone.

"Would you stop worrying? It's just a surface scratch. He was probably crying more from exhaustion than pain."

"Really?"

"Yep. And those little snaps on the shoulder of his outfit? Anybody could have missed them."

"Oh, sure." Cynthia flopped back against the pillow on Tiffany's bed and watched Rick rock Hondo.

Bottom outthrust, the child was seated on Rick's forearm, sound asleep against his broad chest. Chubby fists were locked in the hair at the back of Rick's neck and his rosebud mouth was slack and drooling slightly. Dark lashes rested upon smooth, round cheeks.

Her heart clutched. Such a little cherub.

"I don't think I can do this." She gave a despondent wave in Hondo's direction.

"Just takes practice."

"Not for me."

"How will you ever survive having your own children?"

"I have no idea. They say it's different when they're your own. I'm banking on that."

"Ah. So. How many kids do you want?"

"Welll, I thought I'd try one to begin with, and if that works...twelve."

"Twelve?" Rick's rumbling chuckle joggled Hondo, but the child didn't seem disturbed in the least.

"Okay, maybe only six. But I want a big family. Lots of people to call my own."

"Have you talked to Graham about that?"

Graham? She hadn't thought of him in connection with her children in ages. Graham had never seemed like the parental sort. She got up and went to the window.

"No. But I…I'm not worried about him. Someday I'll have a bunch of children." She could feel Rick's gaze on her back as she stared out the window. "I was an only child. In and out of foster care. It was lonely. Very lonely."

The rocker slowed and Cynthia turned.

"I can identify with the lonely part," he said softly.

"You have a mom and dad."

"And a brother."

She looked into his eyes. "And a brother."

"A real nuclear family. Such as they are." He shrugged. "When I was growing up, they meant well, but there was a lot lacking."

"Lacking? That's funny. I'd never have said that about the Wingates."

"Money can't buy parental instincts. And though Mom and Dad are really great people, and dote on each other, they were pretty clueless about raising the little hellion boys they managed to spawn. I think they solved the situation by keeping us in boarding schools and farming us out to summer camps and relatives.

"So, though I had a mother and father to call my own, I didn't really know them on more than a superficial level. Still don't. That was lonely. Graham felt it even more keenly than I did. He's still trying to impress Dad with the fact that he's worthy of the Wingate moniker. I think he still fantasizes that one day Dad will ask him to go out and toss the ball around." Brow quirked, Rick sighed. "Ain't gonna happen. Harrison's not that kind of guy. And Graham needs to accept that. And grow up. Take responsibility for…"

Seeming to feel that he was out of line, Rick stopped. "Sorry. I know he's your fiancé and everything—"

"Oh, no. He's...that's okay."

Hondo stirred in Rick's arms and, chin to chest, Rick peered into the sleeping face. "He's cute."

Cynthia emitted a soft huff. "Now."

Gently Rick lowered his lips to the baby's forehead and kissed his brow. "And he smells like talc." A cloud of dust wafted as he patted the little rear end.

"I'm learning."

Cheek lolling on the baby's head, he peered up at her and smiled. "You are."

The contrast of the powerful man and the tiny child brought a lump to Cynthia's throat. He really was a neat man. So gentle and sweet with the baby. Hondo had stopped crying the moment Rick had taken him in his arms and begun to rub his back. Cynthia knew the feeling. Rick Wingate exuded a strength that was so comforting. He must certainly make a wonderful doctor to those hurting and in need. As she watched him rock the child, it was easy to envision parenting children with him. Curiously, something she'd never really pictured with Graham.

It was easy to picture all manner of things she never had with Graham.

At exactly five minutes to nine Tiffany clomped through the front door of Cynthia's mansion and slammed it shut.

"Cyn?" She paused in the entryway long enough to shove Alfred's old fatigue jacket into the hall closet. "Anybody home?" She tossed several bags into the back of the closet, where Cynthia wouldn't find them, and then kicked the door closed. "Hey, everybody. I'm home."

Hand to railing, she skipped up the staircase and headed toward her room. "Cyn? Hondo?" she called into the silence. She peeked first into her room, then, upon seeing it empty, stepped down the hall to Cynthia's room.

It was there she found Cynthia curled on Alfred's old bed, spooned with Hondo at her tummy and Rick snoring softly at her back. The bed was covered with toys and books and it looked as if they'd all fallen asleep while playing with Hondo.

Tiffany grinned. "Hey, Ricky, he's so fine," she whispered as she pulled the comforter from the end of the bed and covered them all up.

Turning out the light as she left, she continued to sing softly, "Yeah, he's so fine I lost my mind, hey, Ricky. Hey, Ricky."

Chapter Nine

Cynthia was in an uncommonly fine mood.

Lips puckered, she blew across the rim of her coffee mug and reflected back over the morning while around her the noisy world of Pudgie's swirled unnoticed. Mmm, yes. Waking up at dawn's first light between little Hondo and Rick had been one of the coziest, happiest moments of her life. While they'd both slept so peacefully, she'd allowed herself to dream that they were a little family, and that this was the way they woke up every morning.

It was a wonderful fantasy, and the warm glow had taken her through the morning rush in a charitable mood.

Until now.

A glance at her day planner suddenly reminded her she was scheduled to take an exam in Latin that afternoon. An exam she was supposed to have crammed for last night. A long tortured groan escaped her lips and she pressed her fingertips to her temples.

"Ohhh, crud."

Why did real life always have to intrude?

Since Graham had left, her course work had plummeted, and she was beginning to wonder if she could pull it out in time to make half-decent grades. She flopped forward onto the table, only to realize she'd landed in a blob of jelly.

Yeech.

As she scrubbed her cheek with a napkin, the unfortunate realization that she wasn't Harriet Nelson blew to bits the last vestiges of her happy reverie. Just who was she trying to kid? She wasn't somebody's wife and mom. She was a hash slinger at Pudgie's.

Daydreaming about a life with Rick was a waste of time.

She tossed the napkin at a trash can, and missed. Everything was such a mess now. Was she going to end up like Grandmother Jayne? Letting the love of her life slip away, because of a bunch of lies?

Dammit, no!

Graham had not kept his word. He was not home yet, and the wedding was slated to begin in less than forty-eight hours. She was through waiting. She didn't owe him anything anymore. He'd broken her trust for the final time.

She was going to spill her guts to the family. Tonight. After Latin class. For a cowardly moment she pulled her lower lip between her teeth and wondered if it would be honest to spill her guts *in* Latin. No. She would begin a life of complete honesty, no matter how scary.

She cast Josh an irritable look as he came in and flopped down across from her at the break-room table. His scowl rivaled the intensity of her own.

"What's wrong?"

"Nothin'."

Heaving a heavy sigh, Cynthia ran her hands over her face and discovered her cheek was still sticky. "I can see something is wrong." She glanced at the wall clock. Since they were alone in the room and she'd already sorted out her problems, she encouraged him to talk. "We have five whole minutes. Spill it."

Josh leaned back in his chair and hefted his huge, teenaged feet up onto the table. "Tiffany and Trent are making me sick."

"Why?"

"He's always pawing all over her and she doesn't do anything to stop it."

"Poor self-esteem."

"Nah. That's not it. She likes him."

"Trust me. Tiffany doesn't have a clue what she likes. Or needs."

"I saw them at the mall last night."

"Jealous?"

"Yeah."

"Why don't you go after her?"

"She thinks I'm a geek."

"That's your self-esteem. You two have a lot in common." Cynthia rested her chin on the mug that now dangled between her fingertips.

"You think?"

"I know. I think you'd be perfect for her. But she won't think so until you think so."

"What should I do?"

"Mmm, now there's a good question. Okay." With a firm thud, she set her mug down, leaned forward and squinted. All the issues she'd been wrestling over the past weeks came tumbling past tight lips.

"First, stop letting people make an emotional hostage out of you. Time to grow up, Josh. Time to stand on your own two feet. Have confidence in yourself. You are a person worth knowing. Worthy of friendship and love. In fact—" as she advised him, her voice rose in intensity, her shoulders snapped back and she began to speak more rapidly "—stop worrying so much about hurting everyone's feelings and go for what you want! You're too young to put up with all this crap. Do the right thing! Now! Before you end up a bitter, lonely old man, in an empty mansion, having spent your life with a woman you never loved, wondering what could have been if you'd only had the guts to do what you knew was right in the first place!"

Josh leaped to his feet, a look of steely determination on his youthful face. "You're right!"

She punctuated the air with her forefinger. "Go out there and tell Trent where to get off. Then tell Tiffany how you feel. What have you got to lose? *Life is too short to throw it all away on the wrong person!* Truth, Josh! Go tell them the *truth!*"

Cynthia suddenly realized that she was speaking more to herself than to the boy, but hey, the same rules applied.

"Yes!" Josh stalked to the door, a man on a mission with destiny.

"Josh, the restaurant is that way." She gestured over her shoulder.

"I know. I have to go to the bathroom and throw up. Then I'm going to go kick some butt."

"Give 'em hell, tiger."

While Cynthia was advising Josh, Rick arrived at Pudgie's. After glancing around for Cynthia and not immediately spotting her, he joined Tiffany at the counter and ordered a cup of coffee to go.

"It's on me." She waved away his money. "Thanks for helping to entertain Hondo last night."

"You're welcome. He's a great kid."

"Yeah. He is."

"Where is he now?"

"Day care. Across the street."

"Ah. Where's Cynthia?"

"Break room. She'll be back in a sec. So, what are you doin' here?"

"Thought she might want to come to the airport with me and pick up some of our relatives who have flown in from Europe for the wedding."

"What?" Tiffany laughed herself half silly. "Why would you guys bother to fly relatives in for this freak show?"

"Pardon?"

"Cynthia and Graham's excellent yet bogus wedding."

"Bogus?"

"Hello? Anybody home? They broke up, bro! Weeks ago. They're not really getting married. Right? Or is it on again? No, please tell me she's not marrying the squid."

"Uh…" Rick clutched the countertop, as the room had suddenly begun to sway. Cynthia and Graham had broken off their engagement? *Weeks ago?*

"You're lookin' kind of Casper. I thought you knew all this stuff." Tiffany bunched her shoulders in a philosophical manner. "Then again, Cyn's not exactly a blabbermouth. I have to *squeeeeze* the juice out of her if I want to hear anything good." Pulling her gum out of her mouth in a long string, she wound it around her finger as she spoke. "So anyway, just so you'll be in the loop, her and your brother are only doing all this wedding thang because it makes your mama so happy. Actually, *Cynthia* didn't wanna do it. He's making her."

Rick licked his dry lips.

"You know she is such a total wimp, she'd, like, give you the bra off her back. She's a mush ball. I think it's because she was so lonely when she was a baby, and she wanted her own mama so bad that she just can't bring herself to tell your mama that she can't marry your brother, the cheating, creepazoid squid. So now she's gonna have to pay for a whole wedding that isn't even going to happen, which is like so twerp, just to save someone's feelings—''

Rick felt his eyes glaze over as he tried to reconcile the words that were coming out of this child's mouth.

"She tried to get your brother to, like, do the deed. But nooo. *He's* the total maggot, if you ask me.''

Tiffany stared after Rick's retreating form. ''Hey, where you going?''

"Tell Cynthia I'll see her later. And Tiffany, don't tell her I was here, okay?''

Nodding, Tiffany pulled her gum off her finger with her teeth. ''You wanna surprise her with the relatives. I get it.''

"Good. Thanks.''

"You forgot your coffee,'' she called.

But Rick didn't hear.

That evening Rick wandered into his parents' family room to find his mother energetically dragging the furniture across the floor, while his father looked on, puffing placidly on his pipe. His mother's aunt, the addled Tante Wally and her hubby, Onkel Fritz, from Frankfurt were snoozing in chairs by the fire, suffering from jet lag and a tad too much cognac. Marcella was seated at an antique secretary in the corner, puffing away on a long brown cigarette and arguing on the phone with the caterer over a mistake in Saturday's menu. Hired help bustled in and out of the room, cleaning, organizing and preparing for the blessed event.

All would have seemed normal on the home front, *if* the damn wedding was actually going to happen. Leaning against a pillar, Rick hovered in the archway and observed the activity, unseeing. All day long he'd pondered what Tiffany had said about Cynthia

And after examining the situation from every conceivable angle, he'd repeatedly come to only one conclusion that made any sense. Cynthia was innocent.

She'd inherited the house because it was Alfred's wish to have someone in Jayne's family enjoy the gift he'd so laboriously created for his one true love. If Alfred wanted her to have the house, then so be it.

He also felt fairly certain that she'd agreed to marry Graham only because, although he could be charming and lovable when he wanted to, Cynthia needed a family. Alfred provided that feeling of belonging. Alfred was a bit of a ladies' man, yes, but he was also a pretty decent judge of character. He hadn't made his fortune by not being able to spot a swindler. Cynthia was not a crook.

And she truly loved his parents. That much was obvious. And they loved her, too.

In all the time they'd spent together over the past three weeks, Rick could not find a single moment where Cynthia had ever acted in any way but selflessly. Oh, sure, she and Graham had really botched this whole wedding deal, but their hearts were in the right place. At least, Cynthia's was. Graham was always a question mark, but he wasn't really part of the equation anymore.

That lifted a boatload of guilt from Rick's shoulders.

Cynthia was a single woman.

Available.

The challenge of making her see that he was the right man for her had the blood singing in his ears.

"Harrison?" Katherine huffed, and paused in her furniture arrangement to glance at her husband. "What do you think of having the pulpit up here between the posts, instead of over there, by the window?"

"Ask Cynthia."

"She's not here just yet. She had a Latin exam tonight, so she's running late."

"Mmm." Harrison nodded.

"I like the idea of the chairs facing this way. That way, Cynthia can come down the stair on your arm, through the foyer, under the arches, behind the chairs and up the aisle, which should be right about…here." She hurled her slender body against the grand piano and shoved it out of the way. "Harry, what do you think?"

"Mmph." Harrison nodded. "Fine."

From the front of the house, the doorbell rang and a staff member's murmur was followed by the familiar sound of Cynthia's voice. Rick tensed. She was here. She was single. She was his. Chin to shoulder, he glanced back at her as she moved through the foyer to stand by him.

"Hi."

"Hi."

"How'd the exam go?"

"Hard to say. I was a bit…distracted."

Lids lowered, Rick cast her a look that he hoped communicated his understanding. And support. And desire.

She got the message and averted her gaze. "Katherine, you look hard at work."

"This? Work?" Katherine's gay laughter bubbled. "No, this is fun! So how was class?"

"Fine."

"Really, darling, now that you are getting married, you should think about kissing all that college nonsense good-bye."

"But I—"

"Cynthia enjoys her studies, Mom," Rick said.

Cynthia darted him a grateful smile.

Upon spotting Rick hovering in the doorway, Marcella jumped to her feet and rushed to greet him. "Rick, honey, you look gorgeous tonight. Hi, Cynthia! Who are you kissing at college?" Her acrid breath wafted with her hearty laughter.

Rick explained. "Cynthia wants to be a foreign-language interpreter."

"Whatever for? Your hubby will only need you to speak to him in the language of love, right, Katherine?" Her long, loud "Hhaaaaa" had them all blinking.

"But I'll always want to work," Cynthia protested. "To travel. To experience life. I never got to travel much as a kid, living in so many foster homes. And now, with all my studies and work, I haven't had any time to vacation. I really want to see the world."

"I think that's an honorable ambition." As he leaned against the pillar, Rick crossed his legs at the ankles and gave his head a bob of encouragement.

"You do?" Cynthia asked.

"Sure. For example, in my line of work there are never enough interpreters. Many times we have to guess at what the patient is trying to tell us. Someone versed in several languages and with a talent for learning new ones could save lives.''

"That's interesting." Cynthia stared at him, a thoughtful expression on her face. "I never thought of it that way before."

"Well, you should. You have the perfect temperament for such work. Not everybody does."

Katherine gave her hands a dismissive flapping. "Now, Rick, don't go putting ideas into the child's head. She's going to stay here and give me some grandbabies. Simply everyone down at the club is getting them...and I—" she grunted "—want...one...too...." Using her legs in order to spare her back, Katherine crouched and circled an enormous brass-and-glass plant stand with her arms and dragged it out of the way.

Nonplussed, everyone simply stood and stared. Where was the Katherine of a month ago, too weak to stand, let alone rearrange the furniture?

Once again Rick understood Cynthia's predicament.

Hands on her narrow hips, Rick's mother surveyed the huge room with a pensive frown. "Harrison, we need to move that pillar."

"Mmm," Harrison hummed around his pipe. "Might be a mistake, dear one."

"Why?"

"Because it's holding up the house."

"Oh, that's just terrible. The sight lines in this room are all wrong for a wedding, unless..." She clapped her hands, rousing Tante Wally and Onkel Fritz, who were more confused than ever upon waking. "I know! We need a quickie rehearsal so that we know exactly where to place the chairs for the *real* rehearsal tomorrow night."

Quickly Katherine explained her familial relationship to the German relatives to Cynthia, then, heels a-clickin', sprang to Marcella's side. "Marcella, dear, you be the minister." She took the woman by the hand and tugged her into position. Spinning on her heels, she pointed at Harrison and Cynthia. "You two stand out in the foyer. Rick, you stand up by Marcella. Tante Wally, you sit… here, and Onkel Fritz, over…here. Now, Wally and Fritz, you tell us what you can see."

"Was sollen wir machen?" asked Tante Wally, wondering what she was supposed to do.

"Ich habe keine Idee," said Onkel Fritz with a shrug.

"Katherine will dass Sie sich hinsetzen und uns erzählen ob Sie alles sehen können." Cynthia passed on Katherine's instructions and guided them to their seats.

Tante Wally was clearly delighted with Cynthia's linguistic abilities. *"Sie spricht Deutsch sehr gut,"* she praised.

"Ja." Onkel Fritz grinned.

"Und sie heiratet unseren Rick?"

"Ja." Onkel Fritz was also under the impression that Cynthia was marrying Rick.

"I…" Cynthia began to explain the relationship, but gave up when Katherine tugged her back to the foyer and shooed her and Harrison up the stairs.

"I'll signal you by singing the wedding march when it's time to come down."

Heady with power, Katherine shouted for some of the staff to hurry in from the kitchen and take their seats, as they needed to test this whole sight-line problem from all angles. When everyone had arrived and was in position,

Katherine nodded at Cynthia and Harrison, and then, through cupped hands, began to hum the wedding march.

"Dum, dum, ta-da! Dum, dum, ta-da! Dum dum de dum dum da dum dum ta-da! Okay, Harrison, lead Cynthia up the aisle to Rick and hand her off to him. Good, good. Now take a step back.... Good, yes, then comes the 'who-gives-this-woman' thing, Harrison does, good, aaaaand sit down. Okay, Marcella, move forward. *Can everyone still see?*"

Thoroughly disoriented, Tante Wally and Onkel Fritz shrugged and nodded.

"Now, Rick, you take Cynthia's hand and turn her to face you, yes, like that, good.

"And, Marcella, go!"

"Where?"

"Give us a little 'dearly beloved' spiel."

"Oh!" Marcella gave her forehead a thorough slapping and laughed. "Okay. Uh, let's see." After a bit of hee-hee-hooting, she sobered and got into her role. "Dearly beloved, we are gathered here to join this man and this woman together in holy matrimony. Sort of." Everyone laughed, even Tante Wally and Onkel Fritz, who were completely clueless.

"Okay, uh, now. Rick, er, uh, Graham, whoever you are—" more giggling "—do you take Cynthia to be your lawfully wedded wife, for richer or poorer, in sickness and in health, in good times and bad, forsaking all others, until death parts you?"

Katherine clapped. "Marcella, that's very good!"

Marcella batted her lashes and said demurely, "I've taken these vows several times myself."

Still holding Cynthia's hands in his, Rick captured her

gaze with his eyes and wouldn't release that hold. In her face he could see a future of happiness. Of love. Of joy. Of children and noise and travel and hard work. And there was nothing in this world that he wanted more at that very moment than to make this woman his partner for life.

"I do," he said clearly, and so firmly that heads all snapped up and looked on with interest. Even Tante Wally and Onkel Fritz.

"Oh!" Marcella brayed. "Gracious. Okay, uh, do you, Cynthia, take this man to be your lawfully wedded husband, for richer or poorer, in sickness and in health, in good times and bad, forsaking all others, until death parts you?"

The ensuing silence was so lengthy that the crowd became a bit restless. Finally a tentative smile bloomed. "I do," she said in a clear voice, never taking her gaze from Rick's.

Again Marcella giggled. "Oh, my. Well, in that case, by the powers vested in me by the Association of Bridal Consultants, I now pronounce that you are husband and wife. Sir, I guess you may kiss your bride."

Now that he understood that she was well and truly single, Rick threw caution to the wind and pulled Cynthia into his arms. She did not resist, the way a giddy bride-to-be would resist such tomfoolery from a brother-in-law, but instead came willingly to his arms and offered her mouth to his, as if this was the moment they'd waited for their whole lives.

Chapter Ten

"Oh, my." Marcella glanced about, taken aback by the kiss that seemed just a tad too familiar. Then, as if hoping her blithe laughter would smooth the awkward moment, she hooted and clapped her hands to signal the end of the rehearsal. "Now, that's what I call throwing yourself into the moment!"

Everyone in the room had leaned forward to stare at the couple in the clinch with the fascinated horror that attracts voyeurs to a train wreck. Clearly, they wanted to look away, but couldn't. Katherine and Harrison clutched each other in the front row, she slumped against him, their faces agog with expressions conveying a "surely he is teasing?" confusion.

Finally realizing that this kiss had taken on qualities for which the world, herself included, was not prepared, Cynthia abruptly pulled back. As kisses went, it had been an eleven on the Richter scale and had left the room shaken.

Hysterical laughter bubbled past her lips and her hands clapped her flaming cheeks.

Everyone in the room emitted a collective sigh of relief. *Aah.* Okay. She was laughing. They'd been horsing around. Brother-and-sister stuff. That was okay. Wasn't it?

Wasn't it? Cynthia also wondered, dazed.

Slowly she raised her eyes to Rick's, and what she found there left her breathless. For reflected in the depths of his eyes she saw love. True and pure as refined gold. And in that millisecond, life as she knew it stopped.

At some point since he'd come home, they had fallen... in love.

Finally coming to terms with the horrible truth, she found herself standing apart, nearly out of body, looking upon this scene with the eyes of an outsider. She was in love with the brother of her former fiancé. And he'd fallen in love with her, thinking she and Graham were still betrothed. What chance did a relationship with Rick have, based on such sketchy uprightness at best?

She'd lied to him from the beginning.

He'd kissed her just now, knowing that she belonged to his brother.

How could she trust a man like this? How could he trust a woman like her?

And, lies aside, heaven help her; she'd fallen in love with a maverick. A man so enamored with globe-trotting that he'd thrown away a close relationship with his family. Rick didn't want a family. He was always trying to run away from family. No. He was not the man for her. No matter how he set her on fire.

"Marry me," he murmured in her ear so that only she

could hear, and she was snatched from her reverie like a fish from a lake.

Katherine, still slumped in Harrison's lap, called out to her son. "Okay, darling. That's fine. Enough shilly-shally. Let's get on with the proceedings."

"Yes, Mom. I am." Again he urged Cynthia in a whispered voice, "Marry *me*."

"Son," Harrison commanded. "Do as your mother asks. Enough clowning around. We only have so much time before the wedding."

"I know." He looked Cynthia deep in the eyes. "Marry me."

Tears welled and rimmed her lower lashes. There was nothing she wanted more than to do just that. But circumstances had rendered the situation impossible.

"I…c-c-*caaan't*," she hiccuped, her sobs making her too incoherent to continue. And with that—and not stopping to pause for her coat—she spun around and ran. The sound of the front door's slam reverberated in the room, further stunning the onlookers.

There was a moment so awkward, so silent and so hideous, everyone in the room ceased to breathe. Finally Harrison found his lungs.

"Richard, I believe your shenanigans have embarrassed our poor Cynthia, not to mention your mother. It's only lucky that Graham is not yet here, to witness such disrespect." After he'd settled Katherine carefully into her own chair, Harrison slowly stood and, facing his son, pointed with the stem of his pipe. "You'd better go apologize, boy."

"Yeah." Rick sighed and rubbed the tightly laced muscles at the back of his neck. He had some apologizing to do.

But that wasn't all.

"What are you doing home so early? I thought you were..." Tiffany looked up from where she was sprawled on her bed in the middle of a Lego pile. Exhausted by the late hour, Hondo slumbered on a pillow, a giant Lego piece clutched in his chubby fist. Clearly, Tiffany had been amusing herself, building an elaborate castle complete with drawbridge. "What's wrong?"

Lego pieces clattering, the teen rose from the mattress and in two strides had her arms around Cynthia, who stood bedraggled, soaking wet and smelling faintly of gasoline.

Haltingly Cynthia attempted to relay the details of her evening as Tiffany handed her tissues.

"He k-k-kissed...me...and he...p-p-proposed to me... I was going to tell the family...that we are not getting m-m-m-married, but I...I...*ran* because...the way he looked at me... I want to marry *him*...but I know I c-c-can't and everyone was *staring* and it was *awful!*"

"It's okay." Tiffany guided Cynthia to a chair in the parlor area, and once she was seated, shoved the box of tissues into her hands. The teen crouched before her and, resting her arms on Cynthia's knees, peered up into her face. "Uh, now, you are all, like, speaking one of those foreign languages or something because I can't *comprende* nada, sister-girl. What—" Tiffany gesticulated as if attempting to communicate in sign "—are you trying to tell me?"

After a moment spent gathering her wits, Cynthia gave her nose a noisy blowing and sighed. "I have just spent the last two hours, trying to get home. I ran out of gas on the freeway. It was—of course—pouring rain. So I pulled over to the side of the road, but didn't realize that the shoulder was so steep. I had to practically rappel my way out of the passenger window and drop to the ground below, where I—'' she gestured to her shoe ''—broke a heel. About half an hour of walking took me to a gas station, where I got a very nice man to lend me a gas can and give me a ride to my car. Unfortunately, the car was tilted at such an angle that more gas poured out than in....''

Tiffany frowned. ''When did he kiss you?''

''Who?''

''Who? I don't know, who?''

''Oh. That. Rick.''

Tiffany squealed, rousing Hondo, who squeaked, sighed and went back to sleep. ''When?'' she whispered.

''During our wedding ceremony.''

''Hello?''

''He was the groom during the rehearsal.''

''He *was?* So, like, now you guys are getting married?''

''No. He still thinks I'm engaged to Graham, and I can't deal with another roving eye.''

''Roving eye? But he doesn't—'' Tiffany craned her neck and peered over her shoulder. ''What's that noise?''

From outside the window, two stories below, the strains of guitar music filtered.

Cynthia shrugged. ''Must be the neighbors.''

''Cyn, the neighbors live in another zip code.''

''True...''

The tune had Cynthia's heart suddenly pounding.

It sounded as if... No. Yes! There were men standing outside singing ''Take Me Out to the Ball Game.'' Leaping to her feet, she rushed to the window. "I can't believe it. He's here to propose to me. Again!"

Tiffany followed, and strained to see over her shoulder. "So go out there and say yes."

"Oh, it's *one, two, three* kisses for you if you'll *marrrrryeeeee meeeee!*" Rick shouted as several men attempted to harmonize.

"Eeeeww." Tiffany wrinkled her nose.

"No! I told you. He's no better than his brother. He thinks I'm engaged to Graham."

"No, he doesn't."

Cynthia glanced back at Tiffany. "What do you mean?"

"I told him you guys broke up."

"You *did?*"

"Mmm. But I have a feeling he already knew. You and squid never really fit, if you get my waves."

Cynthia turned to again peer out the window and raw emotions—love, relief, sorrow, fear and pride—warred within as she watched this lovely man standing in the pouring rain with a dozen roses and a bottle of wine. If her eyes weren't playing tricks, she could almost swear that was Phillip Michael Allen playing the guitar, and the two Dieters were holding umbrellas and singing backup.

"What are you doing?" Tiffany asked as Cynthia pushed off the windowsill and headed out the door.

"I wish I knew," she muttered past the lump in her throat.

Cynthia pushed through the massive mahogany doors of Alfred's mansion and moved across the porch and down the front stairs. Rain went unnoticed as it pelted her face, mingling with her tears and causing her already damp clothing to cling to her body.

"What are you *doing?*" she shouted over the combined din of weather and music.

With his hand, Rick gestured for the men behind him to stop singing and head for shelter. Happily they rushed to his car.

Rick walked slowly across the driveway to stand before her. "I want you to marry me."

"But...but..." she blubbered, "I can't."

"Why?"

"Because I've done nothing but lie to you since the moment we met." Cynthia inhaled raggedly and sobbed. "And I'm so sorry. The truth is, I'm not going to marry Graham. I don't think I ever really loved him. I...I...and then I inherited the stupid house out from under your parents and all I ever wanted was...a m-m-mother and a f-f-father and I was so afraid they'd *hate* me...if I didn't marry Graham and t-t-took the house away."

"Shhh. I know. And I understand." Reaching out, he pulled her into his arms and kissed her temple. "Don't cry, sweetheart. I'd have probably done the same thing myself. I know you love my parents and would do anything for them. Including throwing away your happiness."

His understanding only made Cynthia sob harder. Her head dropped against his chest, muffling her words. "I never really loved Graham, but I didn't really know it, until you—" She lifted her face up to his, ignoring the rain, and sighed. "Until you."

With the tips of his fingers Rick brushed the rain from her eyes and cheeks. Then, where his fingers had been, his lips lightly trailed. The light of love in his eyes was clear and strong as he leaned back and forced her to meet his gaze by tipping her chin with his thumb.

He sighed, and for a moment groped for words. "Cynthia, our grandparents were, each in their own ways, so obstinate, they lost out on their one true love. Are you willing to do that?"

Cynthia sniffed. "No."

"Then marry me. I love you."

She went very still. "Oh, Rick. I love you, too, but we have so many problems."

"Name one we can't overcome together."

"You don't want a family."

"Whatever gave you that insane idea?"

"You are always running away from yours."

Laughter rumbled in Rick's chest. "Cynthia, I have a job to do. Yes, it takes me away from my family. But that doesn't mean I don't love them."

"It—" she sniffed "—doesn't?"

"No. But it does mean that I can't *live* with them. At least not for very long. I love my wacky folks and my brother, too, misguided as he is at times. But I want a family I can call my own. Starting with—" he lowered his lips to hers "—a woman I can call my own."

She murmured against his mouth. "What about Graham?"

"He'll survive."

Cynthia grinned. "True. What about Alfred's house?"

"What do you want to do with it?"

Forehead together with his, she said, "I...I've been thinking of sharing it."

"With who?"

"A charity."

"Such as?"

"Well, I figured I'd—or whoever—"

"Whoever?"

"Maybe you?"

He pressed his mouth to hers. "Maybe me."

She giggled. "You're distracting me. Anyway, *we'd* move to the gatehouse and turn the big house into a home for unwed teenaged mothers."

"Mmm. Good idea. Okay by me. That way we can spend part of the year overseas with West Coast Emergency Medical Teams." He nuzzled her face with his nose. "They need interpreters," he cajoled.

"That sounds…interesting." Laughter mingled with relief and happiness swirled in Cynthia's belly to rise in her throat and finally escape in a burst of glee. "Okay, then, yes."

"Yes?"

"Yes!"

"Yesssss!" Rick shouted, and, sweeping Cynthia off her feet, spun her in circles.

The expression on Tiffany's face, pressed to the glass two stories above, went from concern to elation.

"Yes," he whispered once again, before closing his mouth over hers.

Epilogue

The day before Christmas Eve arrived along with a light sprinkling of snow. Katherine's house was decorated to the hilt and jam-packed with friends and relatives bearing gifts. Marcella, smoking like a chimney, barked orders at the wedding party in a stage whisper from the foyer. The guests—assembled in the "chapel" Katherine had fashioned in the family room—conversed in low murmurs while waiting for the proceedings to begin. Low Christmas music was piped in through the house's stereo and every room flickered with candlelight.

Graham, having only just arrived that morning from France, was finally in his tux and ready to go. Cynthia waited with Harrison at the top of the stairs, nervously smoothing her skirts, while Tiffany hung over the balcony in her surprisingly sedate prom dress, watching for Marcella's cue.

It had been announced only moments ago by Alfred's lawyer that the final fate of the Wingate mansion had been decided and would be revealed at the reception—held up on the hill at the mansion—right after the wedding. Many of the guests had been at the reading of the will, and were eagerly awaiting the moment. Had there been some mistake in the will? Was Cynthia not the inheritor after all? Perhaps Alfred had looked kindly upon one of them?

The sense of anticipation in the room was tangible.

The Christmas music faded and the first chords of the wedding march were struck. Excitedly, Tiffany whirled and clasped Cynthia's hands in her own. "Good luck," she whispered, then turned and descended the stairs. When she reached the bottom, she waved at Josh through the viewfinder of his video camera, and blew kisses. "See you later at the reception, babe." The picture shook, bobbed twice and then turned to focus on the task at hand.

Graham and Rick stepped up to the altar area and turned to face the crowd. Then Cynthia, on Harrison's arm, began her journey down the sweeping stairs to meet her husband-to-be. When she arrived at the end of the aisle, the minister asked, "Who gives this woman in marriage?"

"In loving memory of her own parents and grandparents, I do," Harrison said. With trembling hands he lifted the veil, his fingers catching in the netting. There were tears in his eyes as he kissed her cheek. "I know you'll make my son very happy."

Her own tears brimming, Cynthia nodded. "I want that more than anything."

Harrison stepped to his seat and settled in next to his softly crying wife, and for a moment, Cynthia hovered, by herself. And then Graham moved forward, grasped Cynthia's hand and led her to Rick, where he joined their hands together.

"There has been a slight change in the program," Graham announced, and a low buzz rippled across the audience.

As Rick and Cynthia turned to face the altar, Katherine

began to fan herself with the wedding program and slumped into the lap of her equally shocked husband. Jaw dropping, Marcella fumbled for her cigarettes and Tante Wally and Onkel Fritz smiled and nodded and dabbed at their eyes.

Graham turned back to Cynthia, gave her one last quick kiss on the lips and then murmured to Rick, "Take good care of her, brother. I love her like a sister."

"I will," Rick said once to Graham and then to Cynthia. "I will."

And for the first time in her life, Cynthia Noble had her family.

* * * * *

Silhouette Romance presents tales of
enchanted love and things beyond explanation
in the heartwarming series

Soulmates

Couples destined for each other are brought
together by the powerful magic of love....

Broken hearts are healed
WITH ONE TOUCH
by Karen Rose Smith (on sale January 2003)

Love comes full circle when
CUPID JONES GETS MARRIED
by DeAnna Talcott (on sale February 2003)

Soulmates

Some things are meant to be....

*Available at
your favorite retail outlet.*

Where love comes alive™

If you enjoyed what you just read,
then we've got an offer you can't resist!

Take 2 bestselling love stories FREE!

Plus get a FREE surprise gift!